'You don't like ... you?'

Jordan gazed at her ...

Claire felt a faint flush of colour creep across her cheeks. 'Don't be ridiculous,' she said lightly. 'I don't know you well enough to pass any opinion.'

'Maybe I'll grow on you,' he said with a slight smile.

'Like leaf mould, you mean?' she suggested.

The smile on his face widened and her heart faltered. How did he do that? How did he manage to quirk his lips into that oh, so appealing lopsided grin? Practice, Claire, she told herself. Years and years of practice.

Maggie Kingsley lives with her family in a remote cottage in the north of Scotland surrounded by sheep and deer. She is from a family with a strong medical tradition, and has enjoyed a varied career including lecturing, and working for a major charity, but writing has always been her first love. When not writing, she combines working for an employment agency with her other interest, interior design.

Recent titles by the same author:

PARTNERS IN LOVE
DANIEL'S DILEMMA

A BABY
TO LOVE

BY
MAGGIE KINGSLEY

MILLS & BOON®

For Patrick and Holly who prove that miracles can happen.

*First published in Great Britain 1998
Harlequin Mills & Boon Limited,
Eton House, 18-24 Paradise Road, Richmond, Surrey TW9 1SR*

© Maggie Kingsley 1998

ISBN 0 263 81243 X

*Set in Times Roman 10 on 11 pt.
03-9810-53685-D*

*Printed and bound in Norway
by AiT Trondheim AS, Trondheim*

CHAPTER ONE

IT WAS a little before twenty to nine when Claire drove into the car park in front of the Ravelston Infirmary. Plenty of time for her to reach the fifth floor. Plenty of time for her to collect her thoughts before yet another fun-packed inter-departmental meeting with Peter Thornton, the head of administration.

Quickly she signalled left, only for her foot to come down hard on the brake.

'What the—?' she exclaimed, as she stared in disbelief at the huge motorbike, sitting in the space clearly marked MEDICAL STAFF ONLY.

'Sorry about this, Dr Fraser,' Andy, the car-park attendant, declared as she rolled down her window. 'If I knew who it belonged to I'd ask them to move it.'

'Can't you just heave the blasted thing into the hedge?' she demanded.

Andy's jaw dropped. 'It's a Harley-Davidson, Dr Fraser. They're collectors' items—'

'I don't care if it's actually Noddy's original bike,' she interrupted. 'I want it moved!'

The car-park attendant shook his head. 'I'm sorry, but the owner's clamped its wheels. It looks like you'll have to park somewhere else this morning, Dr Fraser.'

Where? she wondered, as her eyes drifted across to the already overflowing public car park. Just where was she supposed to park? The whole point of them having designated spaces was so that the Ravelston's staff didn't end up half a mile away from the hospital.

Without a word she wrenched the gear-lever and reversed—only to hear the ominous sound of breaking glass.

5

A quick glance over her shoulder confirmed the worst. She'd backed straight into Peter Thornton's immaculate BMW.

'It's not too bad, Dr Fraser,' Andy observed encouragingly as she leaned out of her window to inspect the damage. 'You've just broken one of his indicators and dented his bumper a wee bit. It could have been worse.'

It couldn't. Peter would think she'd done it deliberately—just as he'd also think she'd meant to be late for his meeting. And she was going to be late—very late, she realised as she went in search of a space in the public car park.

'Oh, wonderful—that's just wonderful,' she muttered, when she finally parked her car and got out to see that it had started to rain. 'Why don't you just send down a monsoon and really make my day?'

With a glare at the leaden October sky she grabbed her briefcase and sprinted to the main building.

'Hold up there a minute!' she shouted as she arrived in the entrance hall to see the doors of one of the lifts closing.

Obediently the doors flew open again and she dashed in breathlessly, only to mutter an oath as she saw herself reflected in the small mirror on the back wall of the lift.

Her shoulder-length straight brown hair was sticking to her face in damp tendrils, her cheeks were bright red with exertion and there were rain spots all over her pale blue suit.

Great, she thought, just great. It would really make Peter's day to see her looking so dishevelled and, without thinking, she stuck out her tongue at her reflection, only to hear a deep male voice declare with amusement, 'You look fine.'

Startled, she turned to find herself staring at a broad, muscular chest. She shifted her gaze up, and then up again, and found a pair of deep blue eyes, regarding her quizzically.

'Are you talking to me?' she demanded.

The eyes smiled. 'I am, and I said you look fine.'

Instinctively she took a step back. There wasn't a hospital in the country that wasn't troubled by weirdos of one kind or another, and the Ravelston in Glasgow was no exception. Security had been tightened lately, but maybe it hadn't been tightened enough.

Yet she had to admit that he didn't look weird. His blond hair might look as though he'd just raked his hands through it, his black sweatshirt, faded jeans, and shabby sneakers might look as though he'd been sleeping in them, but he didn't look weird. In fact, she thought with a disturbing lurch of her heart, he looked rather nice.

And since when did you become such an expert on men, Claire Fraser? a little voice whispered. You couldn't even prevent your own husband from going off with someone else. This man could be an axe murderer or a convicted rapist for all you know.

'I'm quite safe,' he declared, as though he'd read her mind. 'I start work here this morning.'

What as? she wondered. A cleaner perhaps, or a porter? Whatever it was, he'd have to smarten himself up, that was for sure.

'Do you work here?' he continued. 'Or are you just visiting?'

'I work here,' she replied coldly, wishing that she'd put on higher heels this morning. At five feet nothing she'd always felt slightly intimidated by tall men, and this man was tall—very tall.

'You're a nurse, right?' he ventured. 'Or a secretary?'

She gritted her teeth. Why did men always assume that if you worked in a hospital you were a nurse or a secretary?

'I'm a consultant,' she said stonily, and saw his eyebrows rise.

'You must be one very bright lady,' he observed.

Now that was a novelty, she decided. Most of the male heads of department at the Ravelston were convinced that she must have had influence in the right quarters to get her job, and it made a nice change to have a man acknowledge that she actually had a brain.

She turned to smile at him, only for her eyebrows to snap down. A pair of motorcycle gloves was sticking out of his back pocket.

'I've a feeling that one of us is going to regret this,' she said with a calmness that was deceptive, 'but you wouldn't by any chance happen to own a Harley-Davidson, would you?'

'Yes, I do.'

'Then you're the bozo who took my parking space this morning,' she exclaimed angrily.

A faint flush of colour appeared on his lean cheeks, and then he smiled—a curiously lopsided smile that was oddly attractive. 'I'm sorry, I didn't know it was your space. I'll move it.'

'See that you do,' she said, as the lift doors swung open on the fifth floor and she got out.

Quickly she began to make her way along the corridor, only to discover with irritation that the motorbike enthusiast had got out, too.

'Now, look,' she said as evenly as she could, 'I'm delighted that this is your first day, and I'm sure that someone, somewhere, is putting out the welcome mat for you so why don't you just run along now—?'

'Has anyone ever told you that you've got lovely eyes?'

She blinked. Was this man serious? She wasn't some giggly schoolgirl who could be impressed by a trite compliment. She was a divorced woman of thirty-one, the acting head of Ravelston's Infertility Clinic, and she didn't have lovely eyes. She had boring grey eyes and yet, as he continued to gaze down at her, she felt herself blushing.

She hadn't blushed for years and it irritated her beyond belief that she was doing it now. Without a word she spun on her heel and walked away, but he didn't go back to the lift. He quickened his step to catch up with her.

'Will you stop following me?' she flared, rounding on him.

'I'm not following you—we just happen to be going in the same direction.'

'I doubt that,' she replied, her eyes cold. 'The fifth floor is reserved for senior hospital personnel only.'

'I know.'

For a second she debated arguing with him and then gave up. She didn't have time for this. If he wanted to get into trouble on his first day then so be it. She strode through the doors leading to the conference room and closed them firmly behind her.

'Sorry I'm a bit late,' she declared as thirty heads swivelled round towards her.

Peter Thornton's eyes flicked to the clock. 'Half an hour late, to be exact, Claire.'

'I really am sorry,' she exclaimed, quickly taking a seat at the crowded conference table. 'Some joker left his motorbike in my parking space—'

'Which is all very fascinating,' Peter interrupted, 'but I'd much rather we got on with the meeting.'

His smile was tight. It was going to get a hell of a lot tighter when she told him about his BMW.

'I believe you were about to make some point, Anne?' he continued, turning towards the head of ICBU.

'You bet your sweet life I was,' Anne Sommerville declared. 'You said that I could have more funding for my intensive care baby unit this year.'

'I said I would investigate the possibility,' Peter replied smoothly, 'but, unfortunately, money's rather tight at the moment—'

'Try telling that to the parents of babies I'm having to turn away!' Anne retorted, thrusting her hand through her thick black hair so that she looked for all the world like an irate porcupine. 'I'm having to transfer them to Newcastle, Peter—*Newcastle*!'

Claire sighed as Anne launched into a spirited defence

of her department. It was always the same. There was never
enough money for anything. She had hoped that she might
be able to persuade Peter to allow her to advertise for another member of staff but it looked as though she might
just as well save her breath.

Dispiritedly she gazed at the opposite wall and found
herself thinking about the man in the lift. He'd had the
loveliest blue eyes she'd ever seen, and as for that smile of
his...

She wished now that she hadn't been quite so rude to
him. OK, so he shouldn't have left his motorbike in her
parking space, and his chat-up technique was as old as the
hills, but she shouldn't have bitten off his head the way she
had. Maybe she could find out which department he was
working in...

She pulled herself up short. Was she insane? Right now
she needed a man in her life like she needed a hole in her
head. When Bob Wilson had left she'd been made acting
head of the infertility clinic on the understanding that the
job would be hers after two years if she could demonstrate
that she was up to it. Well, she still had another nine months
to go and she wasn't about to muck up her chances no
matter how appealing some man's smile might be.

'We appear to be boring you, Claire.'

A deep flush of colour crept across her cheeks as she
glanced round to find Peter's eyes on her, and a ripple of
laughter ran round the table. Damn and blast that man in
the lift. If she hadn't been thinking about him she wouldn't
have left herself wide open for one of Peter's jibes.

And he did so enjoy making her look unprofessional.
Ever since that night when he'd caught her alone in her
consulting room, and she'd had to show him in no uncertain
terms that when a girl said no she meant no, Peter had been
out to get her.

Determinedly she lifted her chin.

'Of course you're not boring me,' she said sweetly. 'How

could anyone possibly be bored in your company? Amazed perhaps, dumbfounded certainly, but never bored.'

The colour on Peter's cheeks darkened for an instant, and then he smiled—a smile that made her wish she'd trashed his precious car.

'That's nice to hear, Claire, especially as I've managed to get you an assistant.'

A frown appeared on her forehead. 'But I haven't inter-viewed—'

'I did.'

She gritted her teeth. 'I prefer to choose my own staff.'

'I know you do,' he declared smoothly, 'but there just wasn't time. The hospital has agreed to employ Dr Marshall for a year—'

'A year?' she protested. 'Peter, infertility treatment takes time—two or three years isn't unusual—and my patients have a right to expect continuity of care.'

'A year, Claire. That's all we can afford—take it or leave it.'

She fought her rising temper. 'Does this Dr Marshall have any experience?'

'He's worked in an infertility clinic in the States.'

Her spirits rose. 'New York? Washington?'

'Wyoming.'

Well, howdy, pardner, and a hip, hip, hoorah, she thought sourly. That was all she needed—some hick doctor from the sticks with ideas that were probably ten years out of date.

'He has excellent qualifications,' Peter continued, hold-ing out a sheet of paper to her.

She scanned it quickly. 'Excellent' was the understate-ment of the year. Dr Marshall had better qualifications than she did, and at thirty-seven he should have been in charge of his own department, not taking up a temporary appoint-ment with her.

'OK, what's wrong with him?' she asked, putting down

the paper. 'Does he have a malpractice suit pending against him in the States or was he caught fiddling the petty cash?'

'There's nothing wrong with him,' he declared evenly. 'Dr Marshall simply wants to work in Britain, but if you'd rather not have him…'

She bit her lip. He was making her look foolish and she longed to tell him what he could do with his Dr Marshall, but she couldn't afford the luxury. She was working a seventy-hour week as it was and still her waiting list remained stubbornly long.

'I suppose he's better than nothing,' she said grudgingly.

Peter smiled again and this time she forced herself to smile back. She hated being beholden to him, but he'd got her another member of staff—albeit temporarily—and for that she knew she ought to be grateful.

'That man makes my flesh crawl,' Anne Sommerville observed with a shudder when Peter finally declared the meeting closed and they all helped themselves to coffee.

'Just remember what I told you,' Claire replied. 'If he tries anything on, one well-aimed knee does the trick.'

Anne laughed. 'Frankly, I'm so short-staffed down in ICBU at the moment that I'd let him take me on his desk if I thought it would get me another member of staff.'

'I'm not putting out any flags yet for this Dr Marshall, believe me,' Claire said with a sigh. 'Knowing how Peter feels about me, I wouldn't be at all surprised if he turns out to be worse than useless.'

'I don't think he will. In fact, I think you'll like him—I know I did.'

Claire paused as she reached for the milk. 'You've met him?'

'Peter introduced me when he took him on a tour of the hospital last month.'

Claire's eyebrows rose. 'A tour that didn't include the department he was hoping to work in. A bit strange that, don't you think?'

'Maybe Peter knew you were snowed under that day and

wouldn't welcome visitors. Or maybe it was your day off and he didn't want you to think he was going behind your back. Hell, I don't know, Claire,' Anne continued, frowning. 'All I do know is that if it were me I wouldn't be looking a gift horse in the mouth.'

Claire's lips curved. 'Talking of gift horses, does the man from Wyoming come complete with stetson and spurs?'

'He's not American—he's English. He's been working in Wyoming for ten years but, apparently, he got a hankering to return to the old country.'

'Couldn't hack it in the States, huh?'

Anne shook her head and laughed. 'Why don't you ask him? There he is now with Peter.'

Claire turned and her jaw dropped. Walking towards her, as bold as brass, was the man from the lift.

'Claire, I'd like you to meet your new assistant.' Peter beamed. 'This is Jordan—Jordan Marshall. Jordan, this is—'

'We've met,' she interrupted coldly.

Peter's face fell. So she'd spoiled his little surprise, had she? she thought maliciously. Well, it was nothing to what she was feeling right now, she decided.

'Hello, again.' Jordan smiled as Peter went to help himself to some coffee.

'I suppose you thought you were being funny?' she observed, ice-cold. 'Not telling me who you were?'

His smile died. 'You didn't introduce yourself either, as I recall.'

It was true, she hadn't, but right now that didn't make her feel any more charitable towards him.

'Now, look, Dr Marshall—'

'No, *you* look, Dr Fraser,' he interrupted. 'And the name's Jordan, by the way,' he added as her eyebrows snapped down. 'I mistook you for a secretary or a nurse, and I'd bet a pound to a penny you thought I was an escaped lunatic or a maniac. We both jumped to conclusions based on appearances, and we were both wrong. Why don't we just call it quits and start again?'

He was right, she knew he was, and as the smile crept back into his blue eyes she could not stop herself from smiling back.

'OK, Jordan,' she said. 'We'll call it quits—and the name's Claire.'

'Any luck with finding some accommodation, Jordan?' Peter asked as he rejoined them.

He nodded. 'I'm moving into a furnished flat in Huntly Gardens next week.'

'Huntly Gardens?' Peter echoed. 'That's where you live, don't you, Claire? What a coincidence.'

It was, and Claire was not at all sure that she liked it. Working with such an unsettling man was one thing—living so close to him was going to be something else.

'He's a real charmer, isn't he?' Anne observed, her eyes following Jordan as Peter bore him away to introduce him to the other heads of department.

'Depends on your taste, I suppose,' Claire replied indifferently.

'Oh, come on,' Anne protested. 'A girl would have to be blind not to see that Jordan Marshall's a very attractive man.'

'Would you like me to have him gift-wrapped and sent down to ICBU?' Claire observed, her eyes dancing.

'If I were fifteen years younger I'd take you up on that, believe me.' Anne laughed.

Claire chuckled and then grimaced as she caught sight of the clock. 'Damn, I've got to go—I've a consultation in half an hour.'

'Just don't jump to conclusions about Jordan,' Anne observed as Claire reached for her briefcase. 'He might surprise you.'

'He already has,' Claire declared dryly.

Quickly she made her way to the door, knowing full well

that she ought to find Peter and tell him about his car. Later, she told herself, I'll apologise to him later.

'Forgotten about me already?'

She started guiltily and then sighed with relief when she saw that it was Jordan.

'Something I can do for you?' she asked.

'I start work here today, remember?'

'Dressed like that?'

The words were out of her mouth before she had time to think, and she found herself flushing as his gaze took in her pale blue suit and cream blouse.

'You'd prefer me to wear something more formal?' he suggested.

'No,' she replied evenly. 'I *insist* that you wear something more formal. I don't want my patients thinking they're being treated by someone who's just wandered in off a building site.'

He grinned. 'OK. I expect I'll find something in one of my suitcases that you'll approve of.'

Her colour deepened. She had every right to be critical of his appearance and yet somehow he had just made her feel petty and small-minded, and she didn't like the feeling one bit.

'Perhaps you could lend me a white coat for today?' he continued as he followed her out of the conference room. 'It'll save me going back to my hotel to change.'

She nodded, but as she led the way downstairs she found herself seriously doubting whether they'd be able to find one big enough.

She was right. Even the biggest white coat that her secretary could scrounge still only came halfway down Jordan's thighs, and as for the sleeves...

'He looks ridiculous,' Roz observed.

'At least he looks like a doctor,' Claire pointed out.

'Like a stupid doctor, you mean,' Roz said with a chuckle.

Jordan glanced from Roz to Claire. 'Do I wear it or not?'

'You wear it,' Claire replied firmly as she went out into the corridor. 'Now, about your consulting room—'

'It's already been organised,' Roz called after her. 'One of the janitors cleared out the room next to yours last night.'

He hadn't just cleared it out, Claire noticed as she came to a halt. He'd also affixed a brass name-plate to the door— a plate that must have been ordered days, if not weeks, ago. So Peter had set her up. Jordan had been going to join her department whether she wanted him or not.

'Something wrong?' Jordan asked, seeing the direction of her gaze.

'Quite an impressive welcome mat after all,' she said dryly.

'Do you mind?'

To her surprise he looked genuinely concerned.

'Why should I?' she answered abruptly. 'Now, you'll have to excuse me, I've a couple waiting—'

'Mind if I sit in—get an idea of how your clinic works?'

For a second she hesitated, but he had to start somewhere and she supposed now was as good a time as any.

If the Bells thought Jordan's appearance unconventional they gave no sign of it. In fact, Claire thought with a wry inward chuckle, they were clearly both so nervous that she doubted whether they'd have noticed if he'd tap-danced in.

'As this is your first visit,' she declared, fixing the couple with her most sympathetic smile, 'perhaps you'd like to tell us a little about yourselves.'

'I'm thirty-seven and Richard is forty,' Mary Bell replied nervously. 'We've been married for eight years and trying for a baby for six.'

Jordan drew in his breath and Claire could sympathise with his reaction. If a couple hadn't conceived after eighteen months of unprotected intercourse then the chances were that they had a problem. What on earth had their GP been doing all these years?

'What sort of treatment has your GP been giving you?' Claire asked, reaching for her pen and pad.

'He gave Richard and me an examination and then he asked me to keep a chart recording my temperature every morning, noting down if I'd got any discharge or a sore throat, or if...if Richard and I had made love.'

'And you've been doing this for six *years*?' Jordan gasped.

'Oh, no,' Mary smiled. 'Just three.'

Deliberately Claire avoided Jordan's eyes. To keep a temperature chart for that long was ludicrous. It was only a guide and many women who were ovulating quite normally didn't notice any temperature drop just before they ovulated nor did their temperature go up afterwards, despite the fact that their ovaries were producing high quantities of progesterone.

'Surely it's vital that we time when we make love?' Richard said uncertainly.

To Claire's surprise, Richard's question was not aimed at her but at Jordan.

'What most couples don't realise,' he replied, 'is that after you've made love a reservoir of sperm stays in the woman's cervix for at least three days—sometimes even longer—so if you make love two or three times a week you're bound to hit the right time if you're actually ovulating.'

'How regular are your periods, Mary?' Claire asked.

'Not regular at all,' she replied unhappily. 'Sometimes they come every twenty-eight days, sometimes they're as far apart as forty days. I know that isn't good...'

'You can still have difficulty conceiving even if your periods are absolutely regular,' Jordan said encouragingly. 'The most important thing to remember is that, although in about thirty per cent of infertile couples the woman can't conceive because she isn't ovulating, non-ovulation is usually one of the easiest conditions to treat.'

The Bells were hanging on his every word and Claire wasn't surprised. His white coat might look ludicrous, and his sneakers were positively disgusting, but even she had to concede that the man exuded authority and ability.

'Of course, we don't actually know yet whether your problem is ovulatory or not, Mary,' Claire said quickly, deciding that it was high time she took control of her own consultation. 'You could have fibroids or scarring in your uterus. Have you ever had any children or a termination?'

Mary shook her head.

'That should rule out a problem with your cervix,' Claire observed, making some notes. 'The first thing I'd like to do is to book you in for a blood progesterone test. It sounds fearsome,' she added as Mrs Bell reached out to grip her husband's hand, 'but all it involves is taking some of your blood to see how much progesterone you're producing.'

'And after that?' Richard asked, his eyes turning to Jordan.

'After that we'll do a hysterosalpingogram,' Claire said, before he could answer. 'That sounds even more frightening but it's really quite a simple procedure. We inject about a teaspoon of dye into Mary's uterus and then take some X-rays. If there's any blockage in her tubes the dye won't go into that area and we'll be able to see where the problem is on the X-ray screen.'

'You'll be pleased to know that we usually call the procedure an HSG.' Jordan grinned. 'For one thing, it's a hell of a lot easier to say after a night on the town.'

The couple laughed and Claire managed a small, tight smile as she reached for her appointment book.

'Would next Thursday be OK for your blood progesterone test, Mary?' she asked. 'And if you could come in then, too, Richard, we could check your sperm count.'

Mary nodded and, after a second's hesitation, Richard nodded too.

It was always the same, Claire thought with an inward smile as she made a note in her appointment book. No matter how modern the man might consider himself to be, he always assumed that the problem was his partner's.

'I think that's all for the moment,' she declared, putting down her pen. 'Now, is there anything you'd like to ask me?'

'But I thought... I mean, aren't you going to give us some pills or maybe suggest an operation?' Richard said in surprise.

'I need to find out what's wrong before we decide on a course of treatment,' Claire said gently. 'Hopefully, it won't be anything major but until we do some tests we won't know.'

Mary Bell cleared her throat awkwardly. 'There's just one thing I'd like to ask, Doctor. I was on the Pill for two years when Richard and I first got married and I was wondering...'

'Whether that had affected your attempts to conceive?' Jordan finished for her. 'Everyone worries about that, but we've absolutely no evidence to suggest that being on the Pill affects your ability to have a baby.' He paused and smiled encouragingly at her. 'The main thing to remember is that you're not unusual or abnormal. Around one in six couples have trouble, trying to conceive.'

Mary beamed back at him. 'Thank you, Doctor.'

'We haven't done anything yet,' he protested.

'No, but I feel a lot better—don't you, Richard?' she said, turning to her husband.

And I feel positively redundant, Claire thought as Richard Bell nodded.

'Nice couple,' Jordan declared, when the Bells had left.

Claire stared at him for a moment. She could cut him down to size. She could tell him that when she'd invited him to sit in on her consultation she hadn't expected him to take it over, but if she were honest with herself he hadn't actually taken it over. It was the Bells who had responded so positively to him and she knew she would have been the same if she'd been in their position.

'You're good,' she observed.

He smiled. 'So are you.' He leant forward and picked up

her appointment book. 'Peter wasn't exaggerating when he said you were snowed under with work. You really do need me, don't you?'

She got to her feet and put the Bells' file in the filing cabinet. Yes, she needed help, but she wasn't at all sure that he was the kind of help she was looking for.

He was too charming for one thing and, though she hated to admit it, his qualifications unnerved her. If she wasn't careful she would start questioning her own ability and that was the last thing she wanted or needed right now.

'What say we go out for a meal tonight?' he continued. 'Celebrate my first day here?'

She took the appointment book from him and put it in her drawer. 'I'm busy tonight.'

'Tomorrow, then—or what about Wednesday?'

'I'm afraid not.'

'Then how about Sunday?' he pressed. 'I'm a stranger here, remember—you could show me the sights.'

For a split second she was tempted and then determinedly she searched through her desk.

'This should help,' she said, handing him a street map of Glasgow.

He gazed down at the map for a moment and then up at her. 'You don't like me very much, do you?'

Whatever else she had been expecting him to say, it certainly wasn't that, and a faint flush of colour crept across her cheeks.

'Don't be ridiculous,' she said lightly. 'I don't know you well enough to pass any opinion.'

'Maybe I'll grow on you,' he said with a slight smile.

'Like leaf mould, you mean?' she suggested.

The smile on his face widened and her heart faltered.

How did he do that? How did he manage to quirk his lips into that oh, so appealing lopsided grin? Practice, Claire, she told herself as he went out of the door and she pressed the buzzer to alert Roz to send in her next patient. Years and years of practice.

* * *

She hardly saw Jordan for the rest of the day. He had said that he'd like to visit the Ravelston's labs and operating theatres before he started work properly and she was only too happy to give her permission. Quite why she was so happy to see the back of him she chose not to consider. All she did know was that by the time she got back to her flat she felt tired and irritable and the frozen meal she had chosen for her dinner had totally lost its appeal.

You could have gone out for dinner tonight, a little voice reminded her.

'I could also have signed myself up for a full course of leg waxing,' she murmured, 'and that at least would have been useful.'

She didn't want to go out with Jordan Marshall. She didn't want to get involved with someone she worked with ever again. That was how she had met Max and look at the disaster that had turned out to be.

Quickly she put her dinner in the microwave, kicked off her shoes, and then pressed the message button on her answerphone.

'Claire—it's Roz. Sorry to ring you at home but the Simpsons have had to cancel their ten o'clock appointment tomorrow and they're desperate to see you. I've pencilled them in for one o'clock—and, yes, I do know that's your lunch hour—sorry!'

Oh, well. She sighed as she poured herself out a glass of wine. I suppose I could do with losing a few pounds.

'Hi, Claire! It's Lucy. I'm having a dinner party on Saturday and I've got this absolutely dishy man coming who would suit you right down to the ground. Do say you'll come!'

Forget it, Lucy, she thought as she switched on the TV. The last time you lined me up with a so-called dishy man, he spent the entire evening telling me how his ex-wife had screwed him for every penny he had when they'd got divorced.

'Hello, Claire, it's Jordan Marshall.'

She whirled round and stared at the answerphone.

'*God, how I hate these infernal machines,*' he continued ruefully. '*I never know whether they're recording my message or not. I just wanted to say how much I enjoyed my first day with you. I know we started off on the wrong foot but I'm sure, if I really work at it, I will grow on you!*'

A smile appeared on her face for a second but it disappeared when she went over to her desk and took out a photograph.

Everyone had said that Max was a gifted consultant, she recalled, and he had been. Gifted and charming and fun. The trouble was that he had wanted a wife and she had desperately wanted a career. For a time she had managed to persuade him that she could do both, but eventually Max had decided that she couldn't and had walked away.

With a sigh she put the photograph back into the desk. Marriage and a career like hers didn't mix, nor did short-term relationships. The minute a man started to feel neglected was the minute the relationship was over.

Slowly she went over to the answerphone and for a long moment she stared down at its blinking red light before she carefully and deliberately erased all the messages.

CHAPTER TWO

NOTHING. Not a whine, not a squeak, not even so much as a whimper.

It was just typical, Claire thought as she got out of the car and slammed the door. Her car would have to play up today when she had such a full schedule ahead of her.

'Having trouble?' a familiar voice asked.

She turned with ill-concealed dismay to see Jordan coming down the steps of 3 Huntly Gardens towards her.

'I didn't realise you'd moved in upstairs from me!' she exclaimed.

He grinned. 'I knew you'd be pleased. So, what's wrong with your car?'

'I haven't got a clue. I'll have to phone for a taxi—'

'No need. I'll give you a lift.'

She stared at him and then dubiously at his motorbike and shook her head. 'Thanks, but, no, thanks.'

'Look, it will take at least ten minutes—maybe fifteen— for any taxi to get here. Add to that the time it will take to get you to the hospital and you're talking half an hour at least. I can get you there in fifteen.'

He was right, and yet...

'Don't you have a meeting with some businessmen at nine?' he continued. 'The ones you and Peter are hoping will donate some money to the clinic?'

He was right again, damn him. She couldn't be late for that, but...

His blue eyes gleamed. 'Go on—break the habits of a lifetime and live dangerously for once.'

She stiffened.

If he had accused her of being too chicken to ride

through the busy streets of Glasgow on the back of his
motorbike she would have admitted it readily, but for him
to imply that she was too strait-laced! She squared her
shoulders.

'Have you got a spare helmet?'

'Now you're talking,' he grinned, opening the box at the
back of his motorbike.

She took the helmet from him and then paused.

'Something wrong?' he asked, seeing her hesitate.

'A simple matter of practicality. A motorbike and a
straight skirt won't mix. I'll have to go in and change.'

'We haven't got the time,' he declared, pulling on his
helmet. 'Just hitch up your skirt.'

'Hitch up my skirt?' she spluttered. 'Jordan, this skirt's
so straight that I'd have to haul it practically up to my
knickers before I'd stand even the remotest chance of getting on that bike!'

'I don't mind if you don't.' He smiled.

'But—'

'I don't see what's bothering you,' he continued as she
gazed at him uncertainly. 'From what I've seen, you've got
great legs.'

So he'd been looking, had he? Well, she didn't know
whether she had great legs or not, but she most certainly
didn't want the world and his wife—not to mention Jordan
Marshall—seeing quite so much of them.

'Look, if it will make you feel any better I'll keep my
back turned while you get on,' he offered.

He was laughing at her, she knew he was, and the an-
noying thing was that she really didn't have any choice.
She couldn't be late—not twice in ten days—and certainly
not when Peter had specially invited people to meet her.

Without a word she pulled on her helmet and then, with
as much dignity as she could manage, she hitched up her
skirt and clambered awkwardly onto the bike behind him.

'Well?' she demanded when he didn't move. 'What are
we waiting for?'

'For you to put your arms around me so that you don't fall off.'

She glared at his broad back. He could make her hitch up her skirt, he could make her look ridiculous, but there was no way he was going to make her put her arms around him.

'I'm fine, thank you,' she declared stonily.

He shrugged and started the engine, but as soon as the bike began to move all her resolve vanished and she threw her arms around him in panic.

'Hey, relax,' he exclaimed with a deep throaty chuckle. 'You're quite safe so just loosen up and enjoy it.'

She didn't feel even remotely safe, and she was certain that she would hate every minute of the journey but gradually, and to her complete amazement, she found that she was actually enjoying the experience. Weaving between vehicles, cutting deftly in front of huge lorries at the traffic lights and then roaring down Great Western Road gave her a buzz she couldn't even have begun to imagine.

'Well?' he asked, looking over his shoulder at her as he drew up outside the Ravelston. 'Was it as bad as you thought?'

She pulled off her helmet to reveal a pair of pink cheeks and glowing eyes.

'It was wonderful,' she breathed. 'It was…it was…'

'*Claire?*'

She swore under her breath. Peter was standing at the top of the steps of the hospital and he wasn't alone. Two smartly dressed businessmen were with him. Two men who could only have been Mr Langton of Langton Electronics and Mr Turnbull of Fernlie Investments.

Swiftly she scrambled off the bike and pulled down her skirt, but she wasn't quick enough. One look at Peter's amazed expression and the equally stunned faces of the men beside him told her that they'd seen considerably more of the head of the Ravelston's Infertility Clinic than they'd ever expected.

'Mr Turnbull, Mr Langton, I'm so pleased to meet you,' she declared, running up the steps towards them. 'Peter's told me such a lot about you.'

'*You* are in charge of the infertility clinic?' Mr Turnbull declared, his face registering clear disapproval. 'But I thought…'

He was staring past her at Jordan, and Claire could understand his confusion. Without his helmet, and immaculately dressed in a dark grey suit, white shirt and blue tie, Jordan looked every inch the head of a department, whereas she— She had a horrible suspicion that she looked as though she'd been dragged through a hedge backwards.

'I know Peter has already explained to you how my clinic works,' she exclaimed, fighting with her mounting colour, 'so I thought a guided tour—'

'Some other time,' Mr Turnbull interrupted, glancing down at his watch. 'I think I've seen— I mean, I think I have all the necessary information.'

'But can't you spare me an hour—half an hour?' she said in dismay. 'I've some figures that I'm sure you'll find interesting.'

'Oh, I think we've seen the most interesting figure already,' Mr Langton said with a smile she did not care for. 'We'll be in touch.'

'Don't go,' Claire begged. 'Look, I can explain—' But it was no use. The two men were already walking away from her.

'Well, I hope you're satisfied, Claire,' Peter said through clenched teeth. 'Three months of coaxing and cajoling, and you throw it all away in ten seconds. What the hell were you thinking of, turning up looking like some…some sort of strip-a-gram?'

'Oh, don't be so pompous, Peter,' Jordan interrupted. 'If two middle-aged men can't take the sight of a bit of leg—'

'A bit of leg!' Peter exploded. 'Damnation, I could practically see her navel!'

'I really am sorry, Peter,' Claire exclaimed. 'I know it didn't look professional—'

'Too right it didn't,' he said tightly. 'And as for you,' he continued, turning towards Jordan, 'get that piece of junk of yours moved. You're parked in a restricted zone.'

For a second Jordan stared after Peter as he stalked up the steps and into the hospital, then he turned to Claire, his lips quirking. 'Was it something we said?'

'It's not funny, Jordan!' she flared. 'And it's all your fault. If you hadn't goaded me into getting on that damn bike of yours none of this would ever have happened!'

'Hey, I didn't know we were going to stop right in front of them,' he protested.

'Well, you should have known,' she threw back at him irrationally. 'I *need* that money, Jordan. I need it badly!'

'There'll be other businessmen, other opportunities,' he said dismissively, 'and I don't think they ever intended donating anything, anyway. I think they just used your appearance as an excuse to get out of the deal.'

'Oh, go…go play on a motorway!' she snapped.

It was his fault, she told herself as she strode into the hospital and along the corridor to the operating theatre. If he hadn't been standing there, looking quite so damned immaculate and professional, she wouldn't have looked so ridiculous, and it was cold comfort to know that she'd been the one who had insisted he dressed that way. And it was obvious that Peter still hadn't forgiven her for hitting his precious BMW.

'Hi, Claire.' Debbie Carlton, the senior theatre sister, smiled as soon as she saw her. 'Something you want?'

'I've come to do Mrs Harding's laparoscopy.'

A frown appeared on Debbie's forehead. 'But I thought Jordan was scheduled to do that?'

'There's been a change of plan,' Claire said tightly as she changed into her theatre clothes.

'Does Jordan know?'

'Does Jordan know about what?' he asked, appearing without warning behind them.

'I thought I would perform Mrs Harding's laparoscopy as I unexpectedly seem to be free this morning,' she said icily.

His eyebrows rose. 'Afraid I might find the procedure too difficult?'

The sarcasm in his voice was veiled but it was there and she forced herself to remain calm. 'She's my patient—'

'Correction,' he interrupted. 'She *was* your patient. Forgive me if I'm wrong but didn't you give her to me, along with the Bells? I might be mistaken, of course—when you've got as many patients as I have it's quite difficult to keep track.'

There was nothing veiled about his sarcasm now and she felt her cheeks redden.

Damn it, it wasn't her fault that she hadn't had time to go through her files yet and allocate some of her patients to him. The fact that she had been deliberately putting it off was neither here nor there.

'Look, I hate to interrupt this…this discussion,' Debbie observed, glancing from Jordan to Claire, 'but Mr Kennedy has booked the theatre after you, and you know what he's like if he's kept waiting.'

'Dr Marshall will do the laparoscopy,' Claire said tightly. 'And, if he doesn't mind, I'll watch.'

Jordan shrugged. Knowing she was in danger of exploding, Claire walked quickly out to the waiting area where a small blonde woman was lying nervously on a trolley.

'Hello there, Liz,' she declared, forcing a smile to her lips. 'All ready for your exploratory?'

Mrs Harding nodded. 'As I'll ever be, I guess.'

'You're not going to feel a thing,' Claire said reassuringly. 'It's not like the HSG, where you had to be conscious so that we could get really good X-ray pictures. This time I'll make sure you're fast asleep.'

'But I thought… I mean, isn't Dr Marshall doing my op?' Liz Harding said uncertainly. 'He said that he was.'

The smile on Claire's face didn't slip for an instant, but inwardly she was seething. She had only given Jordan the case ten days ago and yet Liz Harding clearly had more confidence in him than she did in her and she'd been seeing the woman for three months.

'How's my favourite patient?' Jordan declared as he joined them.

'Fine, Doctor, just fine,' Liz beamed.

'I've just got one or two questions to ask and then we'll get this show on the road,' Jordan continued. 'When did your last period finish?'

'Five days ago.'

'Any vaginal discharge recently?'

'No.'

'Any pain when you and your husband make love?'

Liz shook her head again and Jordan smiled. 'Relax. I haven't lost a patient yet and I don't aim for you to be the first.'

Within seconds Bill Morton had Liz anaesthetised, and Claire watched critically as Jordan made his first tiny incisions.

He was good, she thought as she watched him deftly insert the tiny telescope into the small cut he'd made in Liz's navel and then expertly manipulate the probe into his second incision near her pubic hairline. Not only did he have great technical skill, he also had compassion and humor.

Unconsciously she frowned. If he'd stayed in the States he could have made a fortune and yet he'd chosen to come back to Britain, without even having a permanent job to come to. Somewhere he must have a flaw, but where?

'Oh, *hell*!' he suddenly exclaimed. 'It's a real mess in here, Claire. Want to take a look?'

He was right. It *was* a mess. Liz Harding's HSG X-rays had suggested that there was extensive scarring and adhesions on her Fallopian tubes, but it was much worse than she'd imagined.

She glanced up at him. 'Are you going to try and separate some of the adhesions?'

He shook his head. 'They're too extensive. I'll take some photographs, but— Damn, damn, *damn*! If only she'd sought help sooner.'

'She did.' Claire sighed. 'Liz and her husband went to a private clinic for five years—'

'Don't tell me,' he groaned as he began to take the photographs of Liz's uterus and Fallopian tubes. 'They paid through the nose and got nowhere.'

She nodded. 'People don't seem to realise that paying for treatment doesn't always mean that you'll get the best care. There are an awful lot of charlatans out there.'

'Why don't they ask the doctor they're seeing if he—or she,' he added quickly with a smile as Claire's eyebrows rose pointedly, 'is also an NHS consultant in a general hospital? It's one of the best guarantees you can have.'

'I'm afraid the sad fact is that most people are so impressed by plush surroundings that they don't think to ask anything,' she replied.

He chuckled as he began to remove the telescope. 'Well, no one could ever accuse the Ravelston of going out of its way to impress its patients with its surroundings.'

It was true. Claire might willingly have matched her team and their equipment against the best in the world, but even she could not deny that the conditions they worked under were far from ideal. The Ravelston was crumbling around their ears.

'Claire?'

She dragged her attention back to the present. 'Yes?'

'About what happened this morning…'

'I'd prefer to forget about what happened this morning,' she interrupted quickly, all too conscious that Bill and Debbie were listening to every word.

'It really wasn't my fault—'

She didn't let him say any more. She just swung out of the operating theatre without a word.

Did the man have no sense, no tact? she wondered as she banged into the changing room. It was bad enough that Peter had witnessed her unorthodox arrival this morning, but if Bill or Debbie knew what had happened it would be all over the hospital by lunchtime.

Angrily she changed out of her theatre clothes but as she began to wash her hands she suddenly caught sight of her furious face in the mirror over the sink and a deep groan escaped her.

What was happening to her? She never used to be so quick-tempered. She never used to fly off the handle like this.

OK, so it wasn't easy to be a woman in such a senior position, knowing that everyone expected you to fail, but a few years ago she would have laughed off what had happened this morning instead of rounding on Jordan.

You're turning into a bitch, Claire Fraser, she told herself. Jordan was only trying to get you to the hospital on time, and he was probably right about those businessmen. If they'd really been serious about donating money to the clinic the sight of your legs wouldn't have put them off.

She sighed. There was only one thing she could do and that was to apologise. As though on cue, the door to the changing room opened and Jordan appeared, pulling off his mask.

'That's got to be one of the worst cases of salpingitis I've ever seen.'

'Go easy when you tell her, won't you?' she urged. 'A lot of women think when you tell them that they've had an infection in the past that what you're really saying is their husband has given them a venereal disease.'

He nodded and then his forehead creased into a frown.

'I wonder why it happens? Salpingitis, pelvic inflammatory disease, endometriosis—they can all be caused by a wide range of common germs that all women carry, and yet only some women develop scarring.'

'And the trouble is that often a woman doesn't even know she's got it,' she observed. 'She might get a vaginal discharge or a period of pelvic pain, but not always.'

'Would you like to sit in when I tell Mrs Harding the bad news?' he asked, pulling off his top to reveal a smooth, muscular chest.

The changing room suddenly seemed curiously airless and she stared down at the sink. 'You don't need me. According to your CV, what you don't know about tubes isn't worth knowing.'

'I'd still like you there,' he replied, leaning past her to get to the soap and revealing that his chest wasn't actually smooth at all but had tiny golden hairs on it. 'She was your patient first, and with damage as extensive as this I think we need to discuss options with her and her husband.'

She swallowed and stepped away from him. 'If that's what you want, OK.'

'Claire—'

'I owe you an apology for this morning, don't I?' she said abruptly.

'Hey, water off a duck's back,' he said dismissively.

She shook her head. 'What I said—about it all being your fault. I was wrong and I'm sorry.' She held out her hand. 'I know this is getting to be quite a habit—me apologising to you—but will you forgive me?'

'Do you have to ask?' he said, taking her hand in his.

Her heart kicked against her ribcage. It was that smile, she thought. He was smiling that curiously attractive smile again, the smile that made her feel so vulnerable, defenceless.

Quickly she withdrew her hand. 'I'd better go.'

'Claire, wait a minute.'

But she didn't wait. She walked out of the changing room and kept on walking until she'd reached her consulting room.

'Pull yourself together, woman,' she exclaimed to the empty room as she shut the door behind her and leaned against it. 'So the man's got a chest that would make Tarzan green with envy and a smile that could charm the birds off the trees. So what?'

He said you had lovely eyes, a little voice reminded her.

She walked over to her mirror and snorted. Well, that was a lie for a start. She had a pair of very ordinary grey eyes, not to mention a quantity of equally ordinary straight brown hair, a nose that was too snub and a chin that was too wide.

He said your legs were great, the persistent little voice continued. Quickly she eased up her skirt and stared down at them. They weren't bad, but great?

'Told you, didn't I?'

She whirled round, her cheeks crimson, to see Jordan's head at the door, a wide grin on his face.

'Something I can do for you?' she demanded, dragging her skirt down fast.

His eyes gleamed. 'And how, but right now I'll settle for a discussion about Mary Bell.'

'Her blood progesterone results were inconclusive, weren't they?' Claire observed, retreating to her filing cabinet and pulling out a quantity of files. 'What did you get from the HSG and the laparoscopy?'

'She doesn't have any cysts but she's also definitely not ovulating.'

'Did you take a tissue sample from her ovaries?'

He nodded. 'I found some eggs so it's not complete ovarian failure, thank God. It just looks as though the eggs aren't being released properly.'

'Hormone therapy, then?' Claire suggested as she sat down.

'That's what I wanted to talk to you about before you shot out of the changing room,' he replied. 'I'd like to start her on a course of clomiphene. Hopefully it will get her pituitary gland working harder and stimulate her ovaries.'

'You don't have to check with me every time you decide on a course of treatment,' she said with irritation, annoyed that he should suspect—correctly—that she'd run away from him. 'I do trust your medical judgement, you know.'

'You just don't trust me?'

His blue eyes were fixed on her with a steadiness that her own heart rate was totally failing to match, but she managed to laugh.

'Not as far as I could throw you, Dr Marshall.'

'Give me time—'

'And you'll grow on me,' she finished for him. 'So you said. Now get out of here—I've got a consultation in an hour and I want to get these files sorted out before my patients arrive.'

'What are you doing?' he asked curiously, gazing down at the files scattered over her desk.

'Picking out which of my patients I can offload onto you.'

Delight appeared on his face. 'You mean it?'

'Hey, why keep a dog and bark yourself?' she exclaimed, and saw him grin.

He made for the door then paused. 'How are you getting home tonight?'

'Bus, Underground or taxi, I suppose. Why?'

'I could give you a lift, if you want.'

Peter would be horrified if he saw her. In fact, Peter would probably want her instantly certified, but maybe it was time she started to live a little dangerously and she had really enjoyed being on the back of Jordan's bike this morning.

'That would be great—unless it would be awkward for you, of course?' she added hurriedly, as his eyebrows rose in clear surprise.

'I wouldn't have offered if it had,' he replied. 'But are you sure? I mean, I thought—'

'That I was much too strait-laced to want to repeat the experience?' she finished for him.

He smiled ruefully. 'Now it's my turn to apologise. Around half past six be OK?'

'Fine,' she answered.

And at seven o'clock I'll get my head examined, she added inwardly as he went out of the door and she returned to her files.

As it happened, nobody saw her riding home on Jordan's motorbike. In fact, it was so dark by half past six that Claire realised she could probably have ridden home in a bikini if she'd wanted to.

'How are you fixed for transport tomorrow?' Jordan asked as he drew his bike to a halt outside Huntly Gardens.

'The garage fixed my car this afternoon,' she replied, still slightly aggrieved that no one had witnessed her act of defiance. 'Apparently, it was just a loose wire or a faulty plug or something.'

'You won't need a lift, then?' he said as he led the way into the building.

For a second she was tempted. It had been fun on the back of the bike and it would be worth it just to see Peter's face but she shook her head regretfully.

'I don't know what time I'll be finishing and it wouldn't be fair to keep you hanging about.'

He nodded. 'Some other time, perhaps?'

'Perhaps,' she answered as they came to a halt in the entrance hall.

'I suppose I'd better go upstairs and make a start on my dinner,' he observed with reluctance.

Ask him in for coffee, her mind urged. You owe him that much after today. But she didn't—she simply nodded and went into her flat and shut the door behind her.

'I don't want to get involved with someone I work with again,' she told the microwave as she switched it on.

'It would make life too complicated,' she informed the television some time later as she sat curled up in a seat, eating her TV dinner for one.

'He's just a natural-born flirt, and nobody in their right mind would want to get involved with a man like that,' she declared as she heard her doorbell ring and went to answer it, only to find Jordan standing on her doorstep, resplendent in a knee-length crimson bathrobe.

'Something I can do for you?' she asked, momentarily thrown.

'I wondered if I could borrow some coffee?' he replied. 'It was only when I got out of the shower that I remembered I hadn't bought any and I could really murder for a cup.'

'Wait there a minute and I'll get you some,' she answered, turning quickly on her heel and striding down the hall.

That's not very friendly, her mind chastised. You should have asked him in, especially as all he seems to be wearing is a bathrobe. What better reason could there be for not asking him in? she answered. The last thing I want is a half-naked man hanging about my sitting room.

'One jar of coffee,' she said as she handed it to him. 'Don't bother to return it—I always keep a spare.'

That was even less friendly, her mind protested as she shut the door on him. I know, I know, she argued, but the last thing I want is for him to think that he can just drop by whenever he feels like it.

She'd scarcely got halfway down the hall, however, when the doorbell rang again.

'Sorry to bother you again,' Jordan exclaimed, 'but I forgot to mention that I'm all out of sugar, too.'

'Sugar?' she repeated.

'Sugar,' he nodded.

Without a word she made her way back to the kitchen.

'One bag of sugar,' she declared when she'd retrieved it. 'Don't bother to return it—'

'Because you always keep a spare,' he finished for her with a grin.

Her own lips twitched.

'Now, is there anything else you need before you go?' she asked. 'A cup to drink it out of, a spoon to stir it with?'

His grin widened. 'Actually, some hot water would be useful.'

Her eyebrows rose. 'Hot water?'

'My kettle's not working.'

She stared at him for a moment and then a bubble of laughter welled inside her and she shook her head.

'Come in and I'll make you a cup.'

'Are you sure?' he asked. 'I mean, if it's any trouble…'

'It's considerably less trouble than all these trips to the kitchen, believe me,' she said with a laugh. 'Make yourself at home—it won't take a minute.'

'Nice place you've got here,' he called from the sitting room as she switched on the kettle. 'Basic would be the kindest word to describe mine.'

'Mine didn't even have any furniture when I moved in,' she called back. 'It's taken me two years to get it looking like this.'

'It must have been tough—starting out again after you got divorced.'

She jumped at the unexpected closeness of his voice and turned to see him, standing behind her. 'Who told you I was divorced?'

'Sybil down in the lab.'

Sybil would, Claire thought dryly as she sidestepped him and reached for a cup.

'Well, to save Sybil the trouble of telling you anything else, I take a six in a shoe and my dress size is a secret between me and my bathroom scales. I like forties and fifties musicals, I'm allergic to oranges and my ideal holiday is two weeks of sun, sand and sea. Satisfied?'

He grinned. 'It'll do to start with. Right, my turn—'

'There's no need,' she interrupted, handing him his coffee.

'You're not interested?'

'It isn't that,' she said, seeing a slight frown appear on

his forehead. 'It's just that I prefer to keep my social life and my working life separate—it's better that way.'

'So you'd rather we just stuck to "hello" and "how are you"?' he said as he followed her into the sitting room.

She smiled as she sat down. 'Maybe we'd better skip the "how are you" bit. If you ask some people that they have a tendency to tell you—and in great detail, too.'

He threw back his head and laughed. 'But how am I supposed to grow on you if we never talk?'

'Oh, I expect you'll survive.'

'You're a strange one, Claire Fraser,' he observed, staring at her over the rim of his cup.

'Strange peculiar, or strange amusing?' she asked, considerably unnerved by his steady gaze.

'Strange unique. With most people you can get a rough idea of what they're thinking from their faces, but you... I haven't got a clue as to what's going on behind those lovely eyes of yours.'

Which is just as well, she thought, because right now what I'm wondering is whether you have anything on under that bath robe or not.

'I wouldn't lose any sleep over it, if I were you,' she said lightly. 'And I do wish you'd stop saying I've got lovely eyes. I haven't got lovely eyes—I've got ordinary grey ones.'

'They're not ordinary,' he replied, putting his coffee down. 'Sometimes they're grey like slate, sometimes they're tinged with blue and right now...' He bent forward and caught her chin firmly in his broad cupped palm. 'Right now they've got tiny flecks of green in them.'

Her breath caught in her throat.

He was so close that she could smell his aftershave. So close that she could see tiny beads of sweat glistening on his chest, but what was more disturbing—much more disturbing—was that she could feel tiny shivers of pleasure running down her spine, tiny shivers that she didn't want to feel.

Quickly she jerked her chin free. 'I think you missed your vocation, Jordan. You should have specialised in ophthalmology.'

'I would have done if I could have guaranteed that everybody had eyes like yours,' he said.

She shook her head and laughed a little shakily. 'You really are determined to make me like you, aren't you?'

He straightened in surprise. 'Am I?'

'You know you are,' she protested. 'All these compliments, the flattery—you never stop.'

'Maybe I just like to be liked?' he suggested.

'Unlikely,' she observed. 'You don't strike me as the insecure type.'

'How do I strike you?'

'Bright, capable, ambitious.'

'Maybe I'm just trying to make a good impression—have you thought about that?'

She considered it for a moment and then shook her head again. 'On someone who is going to be your boss for just a year? I don't think so.'

His gaze caught and held hers. 'Who said anything about wanting to impress you professionally?'

Her stomach contracted, and she could hear her heart drumming in her ears, but she managed to smile.

'Oh, I like that one, Jordan. I'd memorise it, if I were you. It might come in useful one day for a more receptive audience.'

A grin spread across his face. 'You always have to get the last word, don't you?'

'Bosses usually do, don't they?' she countered lightly, and saw his grin deepen. 'Have you finished your coffee?'

One eyebrow quirked. 'Is that a hint for me to go?'

'Got it in one,' she laughed, getting to her feet.

'Thanks for the coffee,' he said as she led the way down the corridor.

Determinedly she resisted the temptation to say, 'any

time', but as he went out of the door another thought came into her head and this one she couldn't resist.

'Hey, Jordan!'

He turned, his eyebrows raised questioningly, and her gaze swept over him appreciatively.

'You've got great legs, too.'

He laughed, a full-bodied burst of genuine amusement.

'You know something, Claire Fraser?' he declared. 'I *like* you.'

And do you know something, Jordan Marshall? she thought as she closed the door on him. I like you, too.

CHAPTER THREE

IT WAS snowing. Large flakes that swirled and danced before they settled into a thick white blanket on the roof of the building opposite.

Jordan gazed down at it for a moment and then sighed.

It had been a mistake, coming here. He should have applied for a permanent post in Britain, instead of accepting this temporary job at the Ravelston, but he had wanted to familiarise himself with the NHS system again and working at the Ravelston had seemed the perfect way to do it. And it would have been perfect if it had not been for Claire Fraser.

He had liked her from the very first minute he'd met her, and if she'd been the supremely confident woman he had originally taken her for everything would have been all right, but she wasn't. She was vulnerable, despite the confident, wisecracking mask she wore. She could be hurt, and he didn't want her hurt as he'd hurt every other woman he'd ever become involved with.

'A penny for them?'

He jumped slightly and turned to see Claire, standing in the doorway of his consulting room.

'I did knock,' she continued awkwardly as he stared at her, 'but you obviously didn't hear me.'

'Something I can do for you?' he asked with an effort.

'I just wanted to know whether you'd still like me to sit in with you when you see the Hardings this afternoon?'

'Please.'

He sounded uncomfortable, edgy, and she gazed at him with concern. 'Are you OK?'

No, he wasn't OK. In fact, he didn't think that he had

41

ever felt less OK in his life, but he forced a smile to his lips. 'I thought our health was a taboo subject?'

'It is,' she said laughingly, 'but I can make an exception once in a while, can't I?'

'I'm fine,' he replied. 'Just fine.'

He didn't look fine, she thought as she went out of his room and along to her office. He didn't look fine at all. In fact, he looked downright miserable.

Be careful, Claire, a small voice whispered at the back of her head. It's just one small step from worrying about someone to becoming involved with them, and you've always vowed that you'd never become involved with a colleague again.

I'm not becoming involved, she replied. I'm only concerned because I don't want him going off sick, leaving me to carry all the work again. Oh, really? her mind whispered. Yes, really, she answered back crossly.

'I've shown Mrs Elliot through to your consulting room,' Roz said as she came out of her office and almost collided with Claire.

'No Mr Elliot?'

Her secretary shook her head. 'Apparently his shift got changed at the last minute.'

It was always the same, Claire thought with irritation. If Alan Elliot's shift hadn't been changed then he had the flu, and if he didn't have the flu then his boss had asked him to work extra hours. In the six months that Alan and Helen Elliot had been registered with her she'd seen Alan just twice.

And she needed to see him. She'd done just about every test she could think of on Helen and had found nothing wrong. Either she was suffering from unexplained infertility—in which case there was nothing they could do—or the problem lay with her husband. But how could she confirm it when she never saw him?

'I'm sorry Alan wasn't able to come in today,' Helen

Elliot exclaimed as soon as she saw her, 'but there was a problem at work—'

'It's all right,' Claire interrupted with what she hoped was an encouraging smile. 'These things happen.'

'But you must be beginning to think that he's not really keen for us to have a baby—the number of appointments he's missed,' Helen continued, twisting her hands nervously in her lap. 'He really does want kids, Doctor—he's desperate to have kids.'

Then he's got a funny way of showing it, Claire thought wryly, but she didn't say so.

'I've got your karyotype chromosome test results back,' she said instead, pulling a sheet of paper out of the Elliots' file. 'You'll be pleased to know that we've found absolutely no chromosomal abnormality in your eggs.'

'That's good, isn't it?' Helen exclaimed.

It was, but it also meant that there was only one thing left to try if Alan Elliot couldn't be persuaded to come in.

'I'd like to do a post-coital test on you, Helen,' Claire declared. 'What I need is a small specimen of your cervical mucus, but I must have it between six and twenty-four hours after you and your husband have had intercourse.'

Mrs. Elliot flushed. 'When would you want the sample, Doctor? I mean, Alan and I... We do make love quite frequently, but with his shifts changing the way they do...'

'Ideally, I'd like it as soon as possible,' Claire said gently. 'Look, I know it's not easy—feeling that you have to have intercourse to order—but it would help me to check whether your cervix is healthy or not.'

And it will also allow me to check whether Alan is actually producing any live sperm or not, she added inwardly.

'I'll try my best, Doctor,' Helen Elliot replied, flushing still further, 'but, like I said, with Alan's shifts changing the way they do...'

Claire nodded and Helen cleared her throat.

'There's something I'd like to ask, Doctor. It might not

be important—it might not mean anything at all—but, you see, I've noticed…'

She came to a crimson-cheeked halt.

'You've noticed what?' Claire prompted.

'It's when Alan and I make love, I've noticed…all of his sperm seems to run out afterwards.'

'Helen, *all* women lose semen from the vagina after they've had intercourse,' Claire replied with a smile. 'It's completely normal. In fact, the more discharge you notice the more semen must have been ejaculated to start with.'

'But—'

'I can assure you that more than enough sperm will get to your cervix and it won't escape from there.'

'You must think I'm a proper idiot,' Helen exclaimed with a shaky laugh.

Claire shook her head and smiled again. 'Of course I don't. I just wish you'd asked me sooner and I could have put your mind at rest.'

The rest of the morning sped by in a round of examinations and consultations, and it was a little after one when Claire came out of her consulting room to see Jordan, coming down the corridor towards her with a broad smile on his face.

'You look happier,' she observed.

'I'm afraid I'm just laughing about something one of my patients asked me,' he replied.

'Let me guess,' she said. 'They either wanted to know whether you thought eating oysters would help them to conceive or if sitting in an ice-cold bath would improve the man's sperm count?'

'Neither.' He grinned. 'What they wanted to know was whether I thought it would help if they adopted a different position when they made love.'

A gurgle of laughter came from her. 'Oh, these old wives' tales! You'd think people would realise that it won't make a blind bit of difference.'

'Oh, I don't know about that,' he observed.

'You're not serious?' she exclaimed. 'You can't honestly believe that if you adopt some outlandish position when you have intercourse that it will improve your chances of getting pregnant?'

He grinned. 'Of course it won't—but think of all the fun you'd have, trying out all the variations!'

Right now she preferred not to.

'Where are you off to?' she asked instead.

'The canteen—they've got boeuf bourguignon on the menu today.'

'I wouldn't get too excited. Today's boeuf bourguignon was probably yesterday's beef Wellington and it will be tomorrow's beef curry.'

'Cynic!'

'Realist, more like,' she said.

'Care to join me—my treat?'

She hesitated for a second and then nodded. 'Why not? It's been ages since I've eaten in the canteen so I guess it's about time I lived dangerously again.'

And it's about time I got used to being in your company, she told herself as she accompanied him down the stairs.

The trouble was that he was such a very likeable man, she thought with an inward sigh. When he flattered and teased her she found it easy to regard him with amused scepticism, but when he forgot to tease and flirt and treated her like an equal then—if he did but know it—she was at her most vulnerable.

'Problem?'

She glanced up at him quickly. 'Sorry?'

'You're frowning—what's wrong?'

'I'm just thinking about a patient,' she lied. 'I've done every test I can think of on the wife, but trying to see the husband is like…is like…'

'Catching an eel?' he suggested.

'That would be considerably easier, believe me,' she said ruefully. 'I think he's terrified that he might be the one with the problem but unless we test him we're never going to find out.'

'It can't be easy for him,' he observed. 'The last thing any man wants to find out is that his sperm count's low.'

'I know, but I can't keep on doing all these tests on his wife.'

'Agreed. Maybe you should—'

She never did find out what he was going to suggest because he let out a groan as he pulled open the canteen door.

'Good grief, Claire, would you look at this queue?'

She peered round his tall form and nodded. 'My guess is that Peter's made one administration cut too many and the entire hospital's decided on a suicide pact.'

He burst out laughing. 'Look, there's no point in us both standing in line. Why don't you get a table and I'll get the food?'

For a moment she hesitated, but she was uncomfortably aware that heads were already turning curiously in their direction and so she did as he had suggested.

She had scarcely sat down, however, when Anne Sommerville appeared at her side.

'Hi, stranger,' she exclaimed. 'I was beginning to think you'd gone off to some exotic Caribbean island with a tall, dark, handsome stranger.'

'Show me where he is and I won't even bother to pack,' Claire said ruefully. 'I've been run off my feet lately, Anne.'

'Tell me about it.' The head of ICBU sighed. 'I'm surprised my staff haven't walked out, with all the extra hours I'm asking them to do. And talking about staff,' she added, her brown eyes fixed on Claire with keen interest, 'how are you getting on with your new assistant?'

'Very well, thanks.'

Anne's eyebrows rose and her eyes sparkled. 'Really?'

'Professionally, Dr Sommerville,' Claire declared, beginning to laugh. 'I meant professionally.'

'So you say.' Anne chuckled and then groaned as her bleeper went off. 'Why does this always happen to me when I'm in the middle of something interesting? Drop by and see me in ICBU soon. It's been ages since we had a talk.'

And it will be ages more, Claire thought as she watched Anne dash away. Good friend though Anne was, there was nothing she liked better than a juicy bit of gossip, and Claire had no intention of giving her anything to work on.

'Sorry I was so long,' Jordan apologised as he placed a tray, laden with what only the very optimistic would have described as boeuf bourguignon, on the table. 'Was that Dr Sommerville I saw you talking to?'

She nodded. 'Do you know her?'

'Not yet, but I'd like to. I've got this pet theory about premature babies and I'd love to discuss it with her.'

'I'm sure she'd only be too delighted to hear it,' she replied as he sat down. 'Just make sure you've got a couple of spare hours before you see her.'

'She talks a lot?'

'No, she cross-examines you a lot!'

He grinned. 'Forewarned is forearmed.' He reached for the salt and then gazed across at her. 'Actually, Dr Sommerville's not the only one who would welcome a little information. How long were you married, Claire?'

She choked over her first mouthful of meat. 'How on earth did we get onto that from premature babies?'

He shrugged. 'My mind works in mysterious ways.'

'You're telling me,' she answered. 'Five years—that's how long I was married.'

'Not long, then,' he observed. 'So, what went wrong?'

'Hey, what is this?' she protested, pouring herself a glass of water and wondering how she could possibly change the subject. 'I didn't realise when you offered to buy me lunch that I'd have to pay for it with reminiscences about my past.'

'I'm sorry,' he said. 'You don't have to tell me if it's too painful a subject.'

'Of course it's not a painful subject,' she replied, unbelievably irritated that he might think she was still hurting because of Max. 'I met Max when I joined the infertility team at the Rochester Clinic in Edinburgh. He was my boss and we fell in love and got married. After five years he decided he didn't love me any more so he left.'

'He went off with another woman?'

'No, he went off with an orang-utan,' she retorted. 'Yes, he went off with another woman,' she said more calmly as his eyebrows rose. 'He found someone prettier and nicer and far less bad-tempered than I was.'

A smile lit his blue eyes. 'I might be persuaded to believe the bit about the temper, but you're never going to make me believe the rest—it's just not possible.'

She stared at him for a moment and then a smile curved her lips. He had a way with words, that was for sure, and even if he didn't actually mean what he said it was nice for a woman to hear.

'Actually, I was lying about Julia,' she observed as she picked up her knife and fork. 'Oh, I'm not being a bitch,' she added quickly as his eyebrows rose. 'Julia was—and is—a lovely girl, but I think her main appeal was that she could give Max all the things that I couldn't. A home, her time, her attention.'

'I don't follow,' he said, puzzled.

She sighed. 'Max wanted me to be his wife. I wanted that, too, but I also wanted a career. I found out that I couldn't have both.'

'But—'

'Oh, Jordan, you know what our work's like,' she broke in. 'We never know from one day to the next what kind of hours we're going to be working, and when it's two doctors married to each other it's impossible. Eventually Max decided that he'd had enough and left.'

'I'm sorry,' he murmured.

'Don't be,' she declared, attacking her meat with vigour. 'It's ancient history now. We got divorced two years ago and I've got a whole new life at the Ravelston.'

'I don't think so,' he said, leaning back in his seat to gaze at her thoughtfully. 'In fact, I think you're still carrying around a whole load of emotional baggage.'

'No, I'm not,' she protested.

'Then how come an attractive woman like you doesn't have a man in her life?'

'Haven't you heard a word I've said?' she exclaimed. 'Jordan, there are four female consultants at the Ravelston and we're all divorced. That's got to tell you something.'

'But it doesn't have to be like that,' he declared. 'Several of the women I worked with in the States had been happily married for years.'

'And I bet the rest were either divorced or had never married.' She sighed. 'Look, Jordan,' she continued as he opened his mouth, clearly intending to protest again, 'something's got to lose out if you want to get to the top in your career, and it's generally your private life.'

He shook his head. 'If you want my opinion, you just married the wrong man.'

She chuckled. 'My mother would love you. She says I just married the wrong man, too. You don't know her, do you? Small like me, with grey hair, and carries a placard all the time with the words "Please Marry My Daughter" written on it?'

He laughed. 'No, I don't know her. Claire, there are thousands of men in the world. If you don't want to risk becoming involved with someone in the medical profession again, why don't you look for someone with a steady nine to five job?'

'Because, if I couldn't make a go of a relationship with a man I at least had a hope of seeing once a day at work, what chance would I have of having a successful relationship with a man I might only see occasionally over the breakfast table?' she replied.

'But—'

'And what's with all this interest in my private life, anyway?' she broke in. 'Why should you care what I do?'

She was right. He shouldn't care, but he knew that he did.

'I guess,' he began slowly, 'I guess it's just that I can see you making exactly the same mistakes as I did, and I don't want that to happen.'

'You've been married?' she said in surprise.

'I was married for seven years before Sophy got fed up with playing second fiddle to my job and left.'

'Then surely you of all people should understand why I feel as I do,' she protested.

He sighed. 'Claire, I've been on my own a lot longer than you have and, believe me, a successful career's no substitute for the feel of someone's arms around you at the end of a bad day.'

'Then how come you've never married again if you think marriage is such a wonderful institution?' she demanded.

A faint flush of colour appeared on his cheeks. 'Because I'm selfish and demanding, and no woman in her right mind would ever want to take me on, that's why. And now we'd better get going,' he added, rising to his feet. 'It's almost two o'clock and we don't want to be late for our meeting with the Hardings.'

He didn't even wait for her. He just strode out of the canteen, leaving her staring after him.

He had accused her of carrying around a whole load of emotional baggage from her marriage, and he'd been right. She did feel guilty about her failed marriage, but she wasn't the only one who was still being ruled by past mistakes. Jordan was still carrying his own particular scars, too.

'Are you sure you don't mind sitting in with me while I talk to the Hardings?' he asked when she caught up with him outside his consulting room.

'Of course I don't,' she replied. 'Sometimes two heads

are better than one, and Bob and Liz are going to be devastated when you give them the news.'

They were.

'You're saying I'll never have a baby,' Liz whispered,
tears welling in her eyes. 'That there's no hope at all because of the scarring on my Fallopian tubes.'

'No, I'm not saying that,' Jordan said firmly. 'What I am
saying is that we're going to have to look at the options
available. Drugs won't help in your case—'

'Then an operation,' Bob Harding interrupted. 'Couldn't
Liz have an operation to get rid of the scarring?'

Jordan looked across at Claire.

'We could do a salpingostomy,' she declared. 'That
would open up the outer end of the tubes, which have become blocked because of the scarring. The operation's done
with microsurgery and, luckily, Dr Marshall is an expert in
this field.'

'Then I'll have the operation,' Liz said quickly. 'If it will
help, I'll have the operation.'

'It isn't that easy, Liz,' Jordan said gently. 'I can unblock
the tubes, but from the photographs I took it looks very
much as though there's severe damage to their linings as
well.'

'Can't the damaged tubes be replaced with plastic ones?'
Bob Harding asked as his wife began to sob quietly.

Jordan shook his head. 'I'm afraid we just don't have
the technology to do that.'

Bob Harding took a slightly uneven breath. 'If Liz has
this operation—this salpingostomy—what would be her
chances of conceiving?'

'In Liz's case, with such severe damage, I would say she
probably has a one in five chance of becoming pregnant,'
Jordan replied. 'But you must remember that it would probably take about two years because of the time it takes for
the tubes to heal.'

'Two *years*?' Liz gasped. 'Doctor, I'm thirty-four and
you're saying I would have to wait two years before I could

even have a hope of getting pregnant, and then it might only be a one in five hope?'

'I'm afraid so,' he answered, 'which is why I think you should consider IVF treatment.'

Claire's head swung round to him in dismay and then she quickly turned back to the Hardings.

'I really would strongly advise that you think long and hard before you consider IVF,' she declared. 'The success rate for the treatment isn't high, and if Liz opts for the operation she would have a chance of conceiving naturally.'

'Only a one in five chance,' Liz mumbled, blowing her nose vigorously.

'The success rate with IVF is even lower,' Claire observed. 'One in eight is about the average.'

'But I thought—I mean, you read such wonderful things in the newspaper,' Bob protested. 'People who have been childless for years, and IVF seems so simple…'

'The technique isn't difficult,' Claire agreed. 'Stimulating a woman's ovaries with drugs to produce eggs isn't usually very hard, and recovering the eggs and fertilising them with sperm doesn't usually present too many problems. The tricky part is ensuring that the embryos stick.'

'Then what about that other treatment—GIFT?' Bob asked.

'Gamete intrafallopian transfer?' Jordan shook his head. 'I wouldn't recommend it for you and Liz. You see, GIFT involves taking eggs from the ovaries, mixing them with sperm and then immediately putting the mixture back into one of the Fallopian tubes. With Liz's tubes being so damaged, there'd be a real risk of an ectopic pregnancy—a pregnancy occurring inside one of her Fallopian tubes.'

Liz gazed at Claire uncertainly. 'You think we should try surgery first, don't you, Doctor?'

'I do.'

'But you would recommend IVF?' Liz continued, her eyes swivelling to Jordan.

'I would, yes,' he replied.

'If we decided to go for IVF, when would we be able to start?' Bob Harding asked.

'I'm afraid that could be a problem,' Jordan began. 'There's a very long waiting list, but if you could afford to pay—'

Claire got to her feet. 'Could I have a word with you in private, Dr Marshall?'

They were scarcely out in the corridor before she rounded on him.

'What are you *doing*—virtually pushing that couple into IVF? You know as well as I do that if Liz has tubal surgery she could conceive quite naturally in a normal menstrual cycle after natural intercourse.'

'"Could" is the operative word,' he observed.

'But surgery offers a chance of a permanent cure,' she protested. 'Dammit, you're supposed to be the expert on tubal damage and you know that in skilled hands it has a much better success rate than IVF.'

'If she only had adhesions around her tubes I would have performed an adhesiolysis and that would probably have solved the problem,' he declared with a calmness that was infuriating. 'But you saw her tubes—'

'I also saw your CV,' she retorted. 'According to that, you consider most tubal surgery a doddle—or was your CV nothing but a pack of lies?'

His face whitened. 'If you'd care to phone Wyoming I'm sure the Granton Clinic would be only too happy to confirm that I quite routinely performed fimbrioplasty and cornual anastomosis ops.'

She blinked. A fimbrioplasty involved completely reconstructing the end of a Fallopian tube, and as for a cornual anastomosis no one but a very skilled surgeon would attempt to cut out the blocked section of a tube and then rejoin it.

'Then I don't understand,' she flared. 'Why won't you recommend surgery?'

'Because her tubes are knackered, Claire.'

Her lip curled. 'Oh, what a wonderfully scientific description!'

'You know what I mean,' he protested. 'Claire, I honestly believe that Liz Harding's best chance of getting pregnant is through IVF.'

'But that's the trouble,' she exclaimed. 'It is only a chance—a one in eight chance. You know the emotional strain IVF puts on a couple. Do you honestly believe that either of them are in any fit state to go through it at the moment?'

'All infertility treatments are nothing more than chances,' he replied. 'And in my medical opinion IVF would be Liz's best hope.'

She clenched her teeth. 'Best hope or the most expensive?'

His face stiffened. 'What's that supposed to mean?'

'Well, I noticed that you were quick enough to suggest they pay for it!' she threw back at him. 'Thinking of the consultancy fees, are we, Doctor?'

Anger appeared in his blue eyes. 'If I'd been thinking of the consultancy fees I would have stayed in the States.'

'But—'

'Claire, why the hell do you think I came back to Britain?'

A faint flush of colour appeared on her cheeks. 'I don't know,' she faltered. 'I've never given it much thought.'

'Oh, but I bet you have,' he said, his lips a thin white line of anger. 'I bet you think I came back because I couldn't hack it there. You did, didn't you?' he continued as her colour deepened. 'Well, I could hack it—in fact, I would probably have become a millionaire if I'd stayed—but what I couldn't stand eventually was seeing only the rich get treatment.'

She looked up at him and then away again.

'I'm sorry,' she said, her voice small.

'You should be,' he declared tightly.

'But I still think you should recommend surgery for Liz,' she said mutinously.

'And I still think IVF is her best option,' he replied. 'And, as you so rightly pointed out,' he added as she opened her mouth, 'I'm the expert on tubal damage so that's what I'm going to recommend—unless you want to pull rank on me?'

She gritted her teeth. She could do that. She could countermand his recommendation, but she wasn't going to. The Hardings were his patients and the final decision had to be his and theirs.

'OK, let's get this over with,' she said, sweeping past him into his consulting room.

'We've made up our minds, Dr Fraser,' Liz exclaimed as soon as she saw her. 'We'd like to try IVF. I know you think we should try surgery,' she added when Claire said nothing, 'but, you see, we're both so tired of waiting. Of hoping that maybe next month I'll be pregnant. With IVF next year we might have a baby of our own. To have surgery would mean that we'd have to start waiting all over again, and I can't do that—I just can't.'

Claire gazed at her with concern. 'You do realise, don't you, Liz, that IVF carries no guarantees? Some couples have had six or seven treatments and still not conceived.'

'I want to try,' she replied, 'and at least this way I'll know quickly whether it's worked or not. I want a baby, Doctor,' she continued tremulously. 'I want my friends to be able to tell me that somebody is pregnant, without being terrified that I'll burst into tears. I want my sisters to be able to invite Bob and me for Christmas, without worrying that I'll be upset to see them with their children.'

Claire sighed. How often had she heard that? How often had women broken their hearts in her office when she'd had to tell them that it might be years—if ever—before they could achieve their heart's desire?

'We can afford to pay for the treatment, Dr Marshall, so when can we start?' Bob Harding asked.

'I'll have to make an appointment with you first to explain what actually happens when you undergo IVF,' Jordan replied. 'If you still want to go ahead after that then there are consent forms for you to sign—'

'Consent forms?' Liz repeated.

'By law each of you must give your consent to the treatment,' Jordan explained. 'You could actually start your IVF treatment on Christmas Eve, but I'm sure you wouldn't want to do that—'

'Christmas Eve is fine,' Liz interrupted, and then turned to Claire. 'Please don't look so worried, Dr Fraser. I really am sure that what we're doing is for the best.'

Claire wished with all her heart that she could agree with them. If the Hardings thought they'd been through hell already, trying to get pregnant, then they were in for a pretty rude awakening when they started IVF.

'It is the right decision for them, Claire,' Jordan said when they were finally alone.

'If you say so,' she replied coolly.

'Claire, tubal surgery is major,' he exclaimed. 'It can take three hours to complete and sometimes the woman has to stay in hospital for a week. She has to take antibiotics to safeguard against infections and then steroids to reduce adhesive formation, and all this with no guarantee of success.'

She said nothing and he came forward a step.

'If Liz's tubes hadn't been so scarred I would have gone for surgery without a second's thought, but they're far too damaged. Even if I did manage to open her tubes there's a very strong likelihood that she would simply have ectopic pregnancy after ectopic pregnancy and that would have devastated her.'

Still she remained silent and he dragged his hand through his blond hair in frustration. 'Dammit, Claire, why don't you say something?'

Her eyebrows rose. 'I'm sorry. I didn't realise this was

a conversation. I thought you were just demonstrating your superior surgical knowledge.'

Anger appeared in his eyes and he gripped his hands together until the knuckles showed white.

'I am not going to lose my temper,' he said through clenched teeth. 'I never lose my temper.'

'Then you're heading for ulcers in a few years time,' she said, reaching for her bag.

'I am not going to lose my temper,' he repeated, 'but there is something I'm going to do.'

'What's that?' she asked indifferently.

'This,' he replied, and without a word of warning he yanked her to her feet, pulled her into his arms and kissed her.

Somewhere in her dazed mind a little voice whispered that she should struggle, kick his shins, punch his chest, but oddly enough her body didn't seem to be listening to those instructions. Her body seemed to be dissolving and melting as he deepened the kiss, as his tongue explored her mouth and his hands slid caressingly up her back to pull her closer to him.

What are you doing? her heart protested, but it wasn't she who jerked suddenly away—it was him.

'I'm sorry,' he said hoarsely, thrusting his hand through his blond hair in dismay. 'I shouldn't have done that.'

'Too right, you shouldn't,' she replied, ice-cold, although her heart was thudding wildly against her chest. 'Kissing your boss might be a novel way of trying to win an argument, but it's not one I'd recommend you to try again unless you want to walk in a very strange way for a week.'

With that she strode out of his room and along to her own and banged the door.

The nerve of the man, she thought as she leaned against the door, all too conscious that her knees were trembling. The sheer nerve of the man! Just who the hell did he think he was?

He's one hell of a kisser, a small voice observed.

'I don't care if he is,' she muttered savagely. 'He had no right to do that—no right at all—and then to have the un-mitigated gall to apologise!'

And that was the trouble, she realised. It wasn't the fact that he had kissed her that was making her so angry but the fact that he had apologised afterwards.

CHAPTER FOUR

'How much weight have you lost now, Gillian?'

'Almost a stone and a half, Dr Fraser.'

'Oh, well done!' Claire exclaimed as she pulled a file from her filing cabinet and sat down.

'I'm thrilled to bits to have lost some weight, of course,' Gillian declared, 'but I still don't see how it's going to help me get pregnant.'

'I've got a confession to make,' Claire smiled. 'We don't know either. All we do know is that sometimes the body's hormone balance can be upset if you're too heavy so it's worth losing a bit of weight to see if it will help.'

'I guess so,' Gillian said, 'but I still think this polycystic ovary syndrome thing is an odd sort of illness. If one in five women have polycystic ovaries, how come one in five women don't develop POS?'

'If I knew the answer to that, Gillian, I'd be sitting on a beach in Barbados instead of being stuck in the middle of Glasgow on a freezing December day!' Claire laughed.

And if I were sitting on a beach in Barbados I wouldn't have to see Jordan Marshall every day and wonder what the hell he was thinking, she added mentally.

She did want to know what he was thinking, she thought as Gillian went behind the screen to get undressed. She desperately wanted to know whether he ever thought about that kiss—the kiss she was finding so disturbingly hard to forget.

If only he would give her some clue—even the tiniest little hint—of what he was thinking and feeling, but it had been a month now since it had happened and not by one word or look had he suggested that he even remembered it at all.

But that's what you want, don't you? a small voice asked. You don't want to get involved with him so you should be pleased that it obviously didn't mean anything to him. I am pleased, she argued back. Oh, yes? the little voice whispered. Then how come you keep sneaking surreptitious glances at him like some love-sick schoolgirl? Because I'm stupid, she answered as she pulled on her examination gloves. Because at thirty-one, with a failed marriage behind me, I ought to know better and I clearly don't.

'There's still something I don't quite understand, Doctor,' Gillian declared some time later as Claire threw her gloves into the disposal bin. 'How, exactly, does the presence of these cysts in my ovaries prevent me from getting pregnant?'

'They don't—not directly,' Claire replied. 'The cysts aren't malignant—they're not going to harm you in any way—but your body senses that there's something alien there so it keeps on producing massive amounts of hormones to try to get rid of it.'

Gillian frowned. 'But I thought women needed hormones to get pregnant?'

'They do.'

'Then, if I'm producing all these hormones, shouldn't I find it really easy to get pregnant?' Gillian protested.

'The trouble is that you're producing too much.'

'But—'

'Look, let me try to explain,' Claire interrupted as Gillian gazed at her in confusion. 'Every woman's ovaries produce three groups of hormones—oestrogens, androgens and progesterone. These hormones are regulated by two further hormones from the pituitary gland at the base of your brain.'

'Blimey, but your body's a complicated bit of machinery, isn't it?' Gillian gasped.

'You can say that again,' Claire said. 'It's those last two hormones—the follicle-stimulating hormone and the luteinising hormone—that influence the development and timing of ovulation. At the moment you're producing too much of them because of the presence of these cysts and so you're not ovulating properly. With luck—if we can find the right drug—we can stop that happening.'

'Wouldn't it be an awful lot easier if you just got rid of the cysts?'

Claire shook her head. 'I don't approve of operating unless it's absolutely necessary—and it isn't necessary unless the cysts suddenly start to grow very big. What I'm hoping is that this course of pure follicle-stimulating hormone injections that I'm going to start you on will do the trick.'

'Fingers crossed.' Gillian smiled as she got to her feet.

'There's just one thing, Gillian,' Claire said quickly. 'Your ovaries are very sensitive at the moment and the last thing we want is for them to become over-stimulated. If you feel the least bit sick, or your stomach becomes even the tiniest bit swollen, you *must* contact the hospital.'

'I understand.'

'I mean it, Gillian,' Claire insisted as the woman opened the door. 'These drugs can be very dangerous if they're not given in the correct dosage so if you feel even the smallest twinge—'

'Contact the hospital right away,' Gillian interrupted. 'I do understand, Doctor. Can I go now?'

Claire stared at her for a moment and then nodded, but a deep frown appeared on her forehead when she was alone.

Gillian White might say that she understood, but she was so desperate to have a baby that she was quite liable to endure any amount of discomfort if she thought she might get pregnant.

Quickly she lifted the phone and dialled Louise Gerard's extension. No matter how determined Gillian might be to ignore the dangers, in a contest between her and the clinic's nurse Claire would put her money on Louise every time.

With Sister Gerard primed to be on the lookout for the first sign of trouble, Claire put down her phone and glanced up at her clock. It was a quarter to eleven. Normally Roz had brought her coffee in by ten-thirty but there was still no sign of it, or of her.

With a frown she made her way along to the office and quickly discovered the source of the delay. Jordan was perched on the edge of her secretary's desk and he and Roz were clearly having a whale of a time.

'Something you need?' Roz asked when she saw her.

'My coffee would be nice,' Claire replied dryly.

'Oh, I'm sorry, Claire,' her secretary exclaimed, jumping to her feet guiltily. 'Jordan and I got talking and...well, the time sort of flew.'

'So I see.'

She wasn't jealous, she told herself as Roz busied herself with the coffee. Why in the world would she be jealous? Roz might be a twenty-five-year-old redhead with a skin like porcelain and a figure to die for, but if she was interested in Jordan, and he was interested in her, then good luck to the pair of them.

And he wasn't her type anyway, she reminded herself, helping herself to a chocolate biscuit from the tin on Roz's desk, although she'd vowed only that morning to lose a bit of weight. Her type was...well, she wasn't exactly sure what her type was but Jordan Marshall wasn't one of them, that was for sure.

'Jordan's just been telling me that he'll be spending Christmas on his own this year,' Roz declared.

'My parents are both dead, and I've no brothers or sisters,' he explained. 'As for friends, it's years since I've been in Britain and I doubt if any of them would remember me.'

They would if they were female, Claire thought, but she didn't say that. She didn't say anything.

'But that's wretched,' Roz protested. 'Nobody should have to spend Christmas on their own. Look, why don't you join me and my friends? We always book a table at the Gloucester for Christmas as a special treat.'

A look of such dismay appeared on his face that Claire almost choked on her biscuit.

'That's very kind of you, Roz,' he declared, rallying quickly, 'but I couldn't possibly impose.'

'You wouldn't be imposing.' Roz beamed. 'In fact, I know everyone would be only too delighted to have you along.'

Jordan glanced across at Claire in mute appeal but determinedly she refused to come to his aid and was rewarded by a look of such deep anguish that it was all she could do not to burst out laughing.

'It's most kind of you, Roz,' he declared, 'but—'

'You'd have a great time—I know you would,' she continued enthusiastically. 'May from A and E is coming and Sybil from the lab. And Michelle from Maternity will be there and Joan from Radiology—not to mention a whole gang of girls from Women's Surgical—'

'I really am very grateful for the offer,' Jordan interrupted, edging his way to the door, 'and I'll certainly think about it, I promise.'

'Just don't think too long, OK?' Roz said as Claire picked up her coffee and followed him. 'It's only two weeks to Christmas.'

He nodded vigorously but as soon as he and Claire were alone in the corridor he let out a deep groan.

'You could have come to my rescue in there,' he said accusingly.

'But why?' she asked with a gurgle of laughter. 'I would have thought most men would jump at the chance to be surrounded by virtually every unattached girl at the Ravelston at Christmas.'

'Not this man,' he said with feeling.

'Chicken!'

'Sensible, more like,' he said.

'But that's not fair,' she exclaimed. 'How come you're

sensible if you avoid situations like that because you don't want to get involved again, and yet if I did the same thing I'd bet my boots that you'd accuse me of being governed by my past?'

'It's not the same, Claire—'

'It is,' she insisted. 'If you practised what you preached, you would have jumped at Roz's invitation.'

'I might have done if I wasn't bad news where women are concerned.'

She began to laugh, only to stop when she saw his expression. He wasn't joking. He was deadly serious.

'That's a bit of a sweeping generalisation, isn't it?' she declared. 'I know your marriage went wrong—'

'And so has every other relationship I've had since,' he broke in, his jaw tight.

'But, Jordan—'

'What are you doing for Christmas?' he asked, clearly anxious to change the subject. 'Are you spending it with your mother?'

This time she did laugh.

'Good God, no. If I spent Christmas with my mother I'd be in therapy for six months!'

'But why?' he said in confusion as they began to walk together along the corridor. 'I know you make jokes about her, but I thought— Well, you seem quite fond of her.'

'I am,' she replied, 'but the trouble is that she and my father were happily married for forty years until he died, and I just can't convince her that times have changed and that I—and plenty of other women of my age—are quite happy living alone.'

'She wants you to get married again?'

She nodded. 'You've no idea how the words, "but, Claire, I only want you to be happy," strike terror into my heart. It means she's dug up some other poor unattached male she's certain will suit me down to the ground.'

He shook his head and smiled. 'That's one situation I've

never had to face. My father didn't give a damn about what I did.'

'But your mother must have cared, surely?' she said, as they came to a halt outside his door.

'Considering she left my father when I was eight and I never saw her again, it would appear unlikely.'

His voice was hard and she looked up at him with concern. 'I'm sorry.'

'There's no need to be,' he said dismissively. 'I survived.'

But not without scars, she thought.

'I'm glad Max and I didn't have any children,' she observed. 'I always think divorce is even harder on them than it is on the parents.'

'It's a whole lot easier than watching two people tear each other apart, believe me,' he said.

'Your parents argued a lot?'

His lip curled. 'Not exactly. My father's answer to every argument was to use his fists.'

Her jaw dropped in dismay. 'He used to hit your mother?'

He nodded. 'And me. When she left I don't know which of them I hated most—my father for his brutality or my mother for leaving me behind.'

Impulsively she put her hand on his arm. 'I'm sure she wouldn't have left you if she hadn't had a very good reason for doing it.'

'Oh, she had a good reason, all right,' he said tightly. 'She just didn't love me enough to want me along.'

'Jordan—'

'It happened a long time ago, Claire,' he interrupted. 'It's part of my past, and it doesn't matter any more.'

But it did matter, she thought. It might have happened a long time ago but the memories were still there—the hurt was still there. She had thought him so confident but there were a lot of unlaid ghosts inside him, ghosts that needed to be exorcised for his own peace of mind.

'Jordan—'

'I've got to go,' he said. 'I'm expecting Richard and Mary Bell at any minute.'

'But, Jordan—'

'I'm thinking of switching her from clomiphene to human menopausal gonadotrophin. What do you think?'

His eyes were guarded, shuttered, and she sighed.

He had shut her out as effectively as if he'd walked away from her. Max used to do the same, she remembered. He would never tell her what he was thinking or feeling, and it used to drive her mad.

'She's your patient so it's your decision,' she said, and then clapped a hand to her forehead in consternation. 'Damn—I've got a memory like a sieve just lately. I saw Peter Thornton earlier this morning and he asked me to tell you that he'd like a word when you've got a minute.'

His eyebrows rose. 'Did he say what he wanted?'

She shook her head. 'I shouldn't think it's anything important—probably just something about your P45. And you'll be quite safe with him,' she added as he frowned. 'Peter's wandering hands are strictly reserved for the divorced female staff at the Ravelston.'

His frown deepened. 'So he's like that, is he?'

'I'm afraid so,' she said with a rueful laugh. 'He seems to have got this idea into his head that if you're divorced you must be feeling sexually deprived and longing to be serviced.'

'I see,' he murmured, his face suddenly uncharacteristically grim.

'Hey, it's no big deal, Jordan,' she said quickly. 'I can handle him.'

'You shouldn't have to,' he said, his brows lowering still further. 'No woman should be subjected to sexual harassment at work. Maybe it's time I had a word with our head of administration.'

'You'll do no such thing,' she protested, suddenly wishing with all her heart that she'd said nothing. 'I'm grateful for your concern—truly I am—but the last thing I want or need right now is a confrontation with Peter.'

'But, Claire—'

'I mean it, Jordan,' she said firmly. 'I've only got this job on a trial basis, and being involved in an accusation of sexual harassment against someone at the hospital wouldn't exactly endear me to the board.'

'But—'

'I'm a big girl, Jordan. I can take care of myself.'

And she probably could, he thought as he watched her stride off along the corridor, but not without it taking its toll on her both mentally and physically.

Even in the short time he'd known her, he could see that she was growing more and more exhausted with every passing day. She might have given him a hefty caseload but he knew from how late she was getting back to Huntly Gardens at night that hers was even heavier.

And it wasn't just her workload that was the problem, he thought with a frown as he went into his consulting room. She was desperate to prove to the hospital authorities that she could run her department perfectly, but he knew from personal experience that perfection was unobtainable in a hospital. There always going to be hiccups, problems, whether the clinic was run by a man or a woman.

A sigh escaped him and suddenly a wry smile crossed his face. He was doing it again—thinking about her, worrying about her—and he had to stop. She was a grown woman, and he... He hadn't been exaggerating where women were concerned. He'd hurt every woman he'd ever known.

'Mr and Mrs Bell for you, Dr Marshall.'

He jumped guiltily. He hadn't even heard Roz open the door, and quickly he affixed a smile to his face as she ushered the couple in.

'How are you feeling today, Mary?' he asked as she sat down.

'Fine, Doctor,' she replied. 'No sign of me getting pregnant yet, though.'

She glanced meaningly across at her husband and he flushed slightly.

'I don't want you to think that we're questioning your diagnosis, Doctor,' he began awkwardly, 'but are you absolutely sure that Mary's infertility is due to her not ovulating? We know her periods aren't regular, but we were reading in a magazine the other day about how stress can affect your fertility.'

Jordan leant back in his seat.

'Stress can certainly affect your fertility, but we've only got to look at women living under conditions of extreme deprivation in the Third World to see that it can't be the only factor. If any women should have problems conceiving then it should be them, and yet they don't.'

'But what about these couples who decide to stop trying for a baby, adopt instead and then have a child of their own?' Richard Bell persisted. 'Surely that would suggest that stress has got something to do with it?'

Jordan spread his hands. 'Like I said, we just don't know but, believe me, in Mary's case the problem is with her erratic ovulation which is why I'd like her to try a course of human menopausal gonadotrophin.'

'Human what?' Richard exclaimed.

'I know, I know,' Jordan laughed. 'It's quite a mouthful, isn't it? You'll be pleased to know that we call it HMG for short, and the newspapers have nicknamed it the fertility drug because it contains a mixture of the luteinising hormone and the follicle-stimulating hormone which naturally stimulate the ovaries.'

'I have read about it.' Mary nodded. 'It's given by way of injections, isn't it?'

'That's right,' Jordan replied. 'We give you the injections over a period of several days during the first half of your cycle in the hope that they will encourage your ovaries to produce several follicles.'

'You mean I could have twins?' Mary said in delight.

'There is a risk that a lot of eggs may be produced in the same cycle, yes.'

'I don't care if I have quads!' Mary beamed.

'But I do,' Jordan said gently. 'Mary, it sounds like the answer to every infertile couple's prayer—having more than one baby—but to have too many can be dangerous for you, not to mention disastrous for the babies.'

'How will you make sure this doesn't happen?' Richard asked anxiously. 'If there's any danger to Mary…'

'There won't be.' Jordan smiled reassuringly. 'I'll arrange for her to have regular blood tests and ultrasound scans so that we can check what's happening.'

'You can do as many tests as you like so long as it works,' Mary exclaimed.

'It might not work—or at least not immediately,' Jordan declared, loath to dampen her enthusiasm, but knowing that he must. 'I've known patients where it's been successful almost immediately but other patients have taken almost three years before we got any results.'

'Three years!' she gasped, her face falling.

'The trouble is that we have to find the right dosage. Too little and nothing will happen, too much and you could be faced with a multiple birth.'

'But three *years*, Doctor?' she murmured.

'I only said that it *could* take that long,' he replied encouragingly. 'I didn't say that it would.'

He very much hoped that it wouldn't, he thought as Richard and Mary left. The Bell's were a nice couple but, then, as he knew only too well, almost all the couples who came to an infertility clinic were nice people.

What was it that a friend of his had once said—that life played cruel jokes? It was true. When he'd worked in the States he'd often passed women in the street made old before their time with too many pregnancies, and yet for so many of the women he'd seen at the Granton Clinic the chance to have a baby was always going to remain an un-fulfilled dream.

Quickly he put the Bell's file away and then stared at the phone. He supposed he ought to call Peter Thornton to find out what he wanted but after what Claire had told him he doubted whether he could be civil to him at the moment.

Unconsciously his hands clenched. It made him furious just to think of that man pawing Claire, hassling her. No woman should have to put up with that, and certainly not Claire. For two pins, he'd sort him out once and for all, but he knew Claire would never forgive him if he did.

He stared moodily at the wall for a moment and then groaned out loud. He was doing it again—thinking about her.

Why was he so interested in her? Good God, he'd even caught himself sneaking glances at her when she wasn't looking, as though he were some lovesick schoolboy. There had to be a logical explanation for his behaviour, but what?

He knew that he liked her eyes. He was fascinated by the way they seemed to change colour all the time, and he hadn't been lying when he'd said that he could never figure out what she was thinking. No matter how often he gazed into them they told him nothing.

Her hair? He shook his head. It was thick and brown certainly but other than that it was unremarkable. Her fig-ure? He shook his head again. She had good legs, but a man didn't find himself constantly thinking about a woman just because she had good legs.

What about her lips? his mind whispered and he felt his groin tighten. He hadn't meant to kiss her, had never in-tended to, and yet he could still remember the softness of her mouth against his and, even more disturbingly, the gen-tle swell of her breasts as his hands had slid up her sides.

He was becoming much too attracted to her, that was the plain and simple truth, and she was too vulnerable for someone like him.

Quickly he got to his feet and went out into the corridor

and across to the office. He had to talk to Claire, and talk to her right now, for her sake as well as his own.

'Has Claire got a patient with her at the moment?' he asked as Roz looked up enquiringly at him.

'Mr and Mrs Reynolds are due in fifteen minutes, but I think she's free at the moment,' she replied.

She was wrong.

Claire was standing outside her room in laughing conversation with a couple who were carrying a baby that could not have been any more than two months old.

'One of your success stories?' he asked when the couple finally walked away.

'I'm afraid not.' She laughed. 'Little Patrick is one of Mother Nature's miracles sent along to ensure that we infertility experts don't get too big for our boots.'

His eyebrows rose and she laughed again.

'Sue and David came to me almost three and a half years ago and I had to diagnose that she was suffering from complete ovarian failure.'

'She must have been shattered.'

'She was. The only thing that I could suggest was egg donation from another woman and she didn't want that.'

'So when did she realise she was ovulating again?' he asked as he followed her into her room.

'She didn't. All she knew was that her periods suddenly started to come every twenty-nine days and her breasts started to get tender just before her period started.'

'And little Patrick is the result?'

'Isn't it marvellous?' she said as she sat down. 'I hate telling women they have complete ovarian failure. There's nothing we can do but send them away, saying that even though they might be sterile now it doesn't necessarily mean they always will be.'

'They must be overjoyed,' he observed.

'Overjoyed?' she exclaimed. 'You'd think they'd just won the lottery—and in a funny way, I guess, they have.'

'You're really happy for them, aren't you?' he said, smil-

ing back at her. 'Is that why you went into infertility treatment—because it gives you such a real buzz to be able to
sometimes help childless couples?'

She nodded. 'When it works it's the most wonderful job
in the world. To be able to see the look on a couple's face
when they finally hold their own child in their arms. Oh,
it's terrific.'

'There's a downside, too,' he commented. 'The times
when it doesn't work—when you have to tell someone that
you've tried everything and there's nothing more that you
can do.'

'But the successes—the successes make up for everything,' she exclaimed, her face softening.

'Why, you old romantic!' he chuckled.

'In this case, guilty as charged,' she said happily. 'Why
did you decide to specialise in infertility treatment?'

'For much the same reasons you did. That's why I went
to the States. I wanted to be at the forefront of medical
research into infertility, and I was, but...'

'The price was too high,' she finished for him.

He nodded. 'The only reason I stayed for as long as I
did was because my wife, Sophy, was an American and she
didn't want to leave her folks. When we divorced...' He
shrugged. 'I stuck it out for another four years, trying to
persuade myself that all the research I was doing was more
important than any guilty feelings I might have, but eventually I just couldn't live with my conscience any more.'

She cleared her throat awkwardly. 'Your wife... Was
she...did she...?'

'Go off with someone else?' He shook his head. 'I think
I could have found it easier to accept if she had, but she
just decided that she couldn't stand me any longer.'

She sighed. 'Our work's got a lot to answer for.'

'In my case, I'm afraid it wasn't just my work,' he said
dryly. 'I'm pretty damn near impossible to live with.'

A deep frown appeared on her forehead. 'Jordan, you
accused me of carrying around a whole load of emotional

baggage because of Max, but I reckon you've got your own warehouse full.'

'Probably,' he said as he sat down opposite her, 'which is why there's something I want to talk to you about.'

Her eyebrows rose. 'That sounds pretty serious.'

'Not serious, just important.' He smiled, and took a deep breath. 'It's about what happened that day in my room.'

She didn't pretend to misunderstand him—there was no point.

'Forget it,' she said quickly. 'It was just you attempting to win an argument in an extremely sexist manner, that's all.'

He smiled ruefully. 'I wish that was all it was, Claire, but it wasn't. You see, the trouble is that I find you very attractive—'

'Jordan—'

'I know, I know,' he broke in as she stirred uncomfortably in her seat. 'We've both been down that particular road before and neither of us wants to risk it again. Correct?'

She nodded.

'But I've been thinking about it, and I don't think we have to go down that road.'

'Don't we?' she asked, letting out the breath she had been unconsciously holding, annoyingly aware that her heart seemed to have sunk slightly in her chest.

'No, we don't,' he said briskly. 'Look, we're both adults, Claire. We both know the dangers and pitfalls of a relationship between people like us, and because we know them why can't we just agree to be good friends?'

'Good friends?' she echoed.

'Just because we like each other—are even attracted to one another—doesn't mean that it has to develop into something sexual,' he declared.

'Doesn't it?' she murmured.

'Of course it doesn't,' he replied firmly. 'And we can make sure that it doesn't develop into anything by avoiding tricky situations.'

'Yes, but—'

'Claire, what other alternative do we have?' he broke in. 'We can scarcely go around, trying to avoid one another for the rest of my time here. I know I shouldn't have kissed you—'

She flapped her hand at him in a think-nothing-of-it gesture.

'But I did kiss you,' he continued, 'and what we have to do now is to face the situation squarely—admit that we like one another, but agree that, for us, friendship is all that's on the cards.'

He was right. Neither of them wanted to put their hearts on the line again, and agreeing to become just friends sounded the perfect solution to their problem. And why shouldn't it work? They weren't teenagers. They were mature adults with enough qualifications between them to fill a couple of pages of A4. If any couple should be able to make a platonic friendship work, it should be them.

She took a deep breath. 'OK,' she declared. 'I agree.'

'Great,' he said. 'And to celebrate our new status I've got another suggestion to make. How about we spend Christmas together?'

'D-do what?' she stammered.

'Look, what's the point of me, sitting upstairs, with my supermarket Christmas lunch for one, while you sit downstairs with yours?'

'I wasn't actually going to have a supermarket lunch,' she pointed out. 'I was going to have roast chicken with all the trimmings.'

'Even better,' he exclaimed. 'I could bring along a melon as a starter and a good Stilton for the pudding.'

'Wow, but that will really keep you stuck in the kitchen for hours, won't it?' she exclaimed, her eyes dancing.

He grinned. 'OK, then, how about salmon pâté for starters and a trifle for a pudding?'

'The local supermarket doing a special, are they?' she said with a bubble of laughter.

'How did you guess?' he laughed. 'Oh, say yes, Claire,' he continued. 'It'll be fun.'

For a second she stared indecisively at him and then made up her mind.

'OK,' she said. 'We'll do it.'

'Wonderful!' he exclaimed, his face lighting up. 'Now, we'd better make a list of what we'll need—the tree, decorations, food—'

'It's a fortnight until Christmas, Jordan,' she broke in, 'and I've got patients due in five minutes.'

'But we've got to start planning—'

'Out, Jordan!' she declared, striding to the door and opening it pointedly.

'Crackers!' he said, as though she hadn't spoken.

'That's exactly what I was thinking,' she observed, her lips twitching.

He threw back his head and laughed.

'To friendship, Claire,' he said, holding out his hand to her.

'To friendship, Jordan,' she replied.

She'd expected him just to shake her hand and then release it, but he didn't. Instead, he drew her closer to him, and her heart began to race.

He was standing so near to her that she could see that his eyes weren't simply blue but had tiny flecks of violet in them. So near that she could see a small pulse throbbing at the side of his throat.

She swallowed. 'Jordan…'

He didn't answer. He simply stared down at her, his eyes warm and a gentle smile on his lips, and then he reached out and smoothed her hair back from her forehead.

A quiver of sensation raced through her, a sensation that increased as he traced the outline of her jaw with his finger.

'Jordan—'

He bent his head and she pulled her hand free from his and stepped back quickly.

'I think...I think I may have just identified danger situation number one, Jordan,' she said, her voice constricted.

The hand that he thrust through his blond hair shook slightly and his voice, when he spoke, was as uneven as hers.

'You're right,' he exclaimed with a crooked smile. 'It might be better if we don't touch, but now you see what I mean about the danger areas. Because we can recognise them we can just stay friends.'

Yes, they could recognise the dangers, she thought as she noticed Mr and Mrs Reynolds, coming down the corridor towards them, but would that be enough of a safeguard? She hoped it would be. She could only pray that it would be.

CHAPTER FIVE

'JORDAN—the very man I was hoping to see!'

A smothered oath sprang to Jordan's lips as he turned to see Peter Thornton, walking down the corridor towards him.

'I'm busy,' he replied, his face cold.

The head of administration looked momentarily disconcerted and then rallied.

'Surely not so busy that you can't spare me just a few minutes of your time. In here be OK?' he continued, pushing open the door to Jordan's consulting room.

For a second Jordan didn't move and then he clenched his jaw and went in without a word.

'Oh, dear, oh, dear,' Peter declared as he followed him. 'This room is quite dreadful. It's dull and poky—'

'It's fine,' Jordan interposed. 'Just tell me what you want, Peter.'

The head of administration blinked and then smiled. 'So you're a man who likes to get straight to the point. I like that. I like that very much. I don't actually want anything other than to ask whether you're enjoying working here at the Ravelston.'

Jordan's eyebrows rose. 'Do you want a truthful answer to that or a tactful one?'

'Why, the truth, of course,' Peter exclaimed.

A faint smile appeared on Jordan's lips and then he nodded. 'Very well. The staff are excellent and the work is very satisfying, but the infertility clinic is run on a shoe-string. It's chronically understaffed and appallingly underfunded.'

Peter sat down with a sigh. 'I'm afraid it's a question of

priorities, Jordan. The Ravelston—like every other NHS hospital in the country—is desperately short of money, and infertility isn't a disease—'

'No, but it's a symptom,' Jordan broke in as he sat down opposite to him. 'A symptom that shows that something has gone wrong with the body. Human beings were designed to reproduce themselves, Peter, and those people who can't do that, and wish to, should be given every help.'

'I quite agree with you,' Peter replied, 'and in an ideal world there would be sufficient money to treat every infertile couple in the country. But we don't live in an ideal world. You know as well as I do that there would be a public outcry if we spent as much money on infertility treatment as we do on heart or kidney transplants.'

It was true. Jordan had lost count of the number of people—and it was always people with children—who had told him that childless couples should be persuaded to get on with their lives, instead of being encouraged to try treatment after treatment in the hope of having a child.

And it wasn't just ordinary people who held these views. It hadn't taken him long to discover that almost all of the heads of department at the Ravelston regarded the clinic as an expensive luxury—a luxury that the hospital could ill afford.

'So Claire will just have to struggle on as best she can?' he said.

'Unless she can attract more private funding, I'm afraid so,' Peter observed. 'And speaking of Dr Fraser—how are you getting on with her?'

Jordan lifted a pen from his desk and turned it round in his hands. 'Very well, thank you. She's an excellent doctor.'

'But perhaps not quite so good an administrator?' Peter suggested.

'Considering the resources she has, I think she achieves bloody marvels,' Jordan retorted.

A slight frown appeared for a second on Peter's forehead

and then it was gone. 'I'm sure she does, but don't you think that the clinic could be managed even more efficiently if you didn't leave us at the end of your contract but stayed on?'

'Of course it would,' Jordan exclaimed. 'Claire would have another pair of qualified hands at her disposal for a start.'

'That isn't quite what I meant.'

'Then what did you mean?' Jordan demanded in confusion.

'Claire is an excellent doctor,' Peter said smoothly, 'and nobody would deny that she has run her department remarkably well since she was appointed temporary head, but the board will shortly have to decide whether that post should be made permanent. Or whether we might be better served if we appointed another, perhaps more qualified candidate.'

Jordan stared at him for a moment. 'What are you saying, Peter?'

The head of administration smiled. 'That I'm glad you're settling down so well with us. Men of your calibre are hard to find, and I think you could prove a real asset to the Ravelston.'

Jordan got to his feet. 'Now, just a minute. If you're suggesting what I think you're suggesting—'

'Those blood test reports you wanted are back from the lab, Jordan,' Roz declared as she popped her head round the door, only to flush slightly as she saw his angry face. 'I'm sorry, I didn't realise you had somebody with you—'

'I'm just going,' Peter cut in.

'Not until we've finished this discussion, you're not!' Jordan exclaimed.

'I think I've said all that I want to at the moment,' Peter replied as he made his way to the door. 'We'll talk again soon, I promise.'

'Something wrong?' Roz asked, bewildered, as Peter

closed the door behind him, and Jordan threw down his pen with an extremely colourful oath.

'How the hell did that man ever get to be head of administration?' he demanded.

'He used to be something important in the supermarket business,' she replied. 'I'm not joking, Jordan,' she continued as his eyebrows rose in disbelief. 'The NHS has changed a hell of a lot since you last worked in it. Admin, finance, even the hospital board itself—they're all run by people with experience of big business now.'

'But a hospital's not a business.'

'Try telling that to the government,' she said dryly.

His frown deepened. 'Where's Claire?'

'She's seen Mr and Mrs Reynolds and now she's putting the finishing touches to her Christmas decorations. Hey, wait a minute, Jordan,' she added as he made for the door. 'I thought you said these lab reports were urgent?'

Another colourful oath was her only reply and as he banged out of the door she put the reports down on his desk with a sigh.

'Doctors,' she murmured with a shake of her head. 'They're all insane—completely and utterly insane.'

Peter Thornton was a worm, a toad, Jordan thought as he strode angrily down the corridor. He had virtually offered him the head of department's job if he wanted it. Well, he didn't want it—not at Claire's expense—and the quicker he warned her about what was going on the better.

Quickly he threw open Claire's door, only to come to a halt in stunned amazement.

When Roz had said that Claire was putting the finishing touches to her decorations he had assumed that she'd meant Claire was decorating a small tree. What he had not expected was to find her perched precariously on top of a decidedly rickety-looking stepladder, pinning paper streamers to the ceiling.

'Claire, will you get down from there before you break your neck?' he exclaimed with concern.

'I'm almost finished.' She smiled down at him.

'In more ways than one, if you're not careful,' he said in exasperation, trying not to notice that her position was affording him an excellent view of a pair of slim ankles and equally slender calves. 'Why the hell didn't you ask one of the porters to do that—or me?'

'Because I'm quite capable of doing it myself, that's why,' she replied, pushing her hair back out of her eyes and shifting her position so that the stepladder swayed alarmingly.

'Claire, will you watch what you're doing?' Jordan cried, and grasped the ladder quickly, only to discover that his action was now affording him a disturbingly tantalising vision of two shapely thighs.

'I'm trying to,' she protested, 'but you shouting at me isn't helping a whole lot.'

'Claire, I'm warning you. If you don't get down from there right this minute I'm going to lift you down!' he declared.

She stuck out her tongue at him. 'You can't. Touching's a no-go area, remember?'

Despite his concern, he grinned. 'Not even if it's an emergency?'

'There isn't any emergency,' she pointed out. 'I've got an excellent head for heights, and this ladder is as safe as houses.'

'Claire...'

'All right, all right,' she said in defeat. 'I've finished what I was doing, anyway.' Quickly she thrust the remains of her Christmas decorations into her pocket and climbed down.

'Satisfied now?' she said, turning towards him.

Anything but, he thought as he gazed down at her laughing, flushed face.

He had deliberately kept his arms as far away from her as possible when she'd come down the ladder so that he wouldn't touch her, but it hadn't helped—it hadn't helped at all. Just her nearness was disconcerting. Just the way her breasts were rising and falling rapidly against her blouse from her exertion was making his pulse race.

He groaned inwardly. How in the world could he ever have thought that he could just be friends with this woman? It was impossible.

'OK, so what can I do for you?' she asked.

'Do for me?' he said, momentarily startled, as he realised that there was one very specific thing that he wanted her to do for him right now.

'Well, you looked like a man on a mission when you threw open the door so I'm guessing that you want a favour.'

He stepped back from her quickly and swallowed hard. 'Not a favour. Claire, Peter Thornton's a worm.'

'I agree totally,' she said in surprise, 'but what's he done to rub you up the wrong way?'

'When you knocked back his advances I think you did a lot more than just dent his ego,' he observed.

'I know.' She chuckled. 'I'd say his groin must have been pretty sore for a few days, too.'

'I mean it, Claire,' he protested. 'I think you've made a very bad enemy there.'

'Rubbish,' she said dismissively. 'He doesn't run the Ravelston—a board does that—and as long as I run my department efficiently there's damn all he can do to harm me.'

'But, Claire, it's not as simple as that,' he insisted. 'You know what hospital politics are like. You only need to antagonise one person, and the repercussions for your career can be horrendous.'

'You're making too much of it,' she replied. 'All I did was what any self-respecting woman would have done. There won't be any repercussions unless—' Her eyes narrowed slightly. 'Unless you know something that I don't?'

He gazed at her silently. How could he tell her that Peter had all but offered him her job? It would shatter her confidence, and as for their friendship... It would drive such a wedge through that, it would never survive.

'Do you know something I don't, Jordan?' she pressed.

'Only what any other man would know,' he declared lightly. 'That kneeing someone in the groin isn't going to make you their flavour of the month.'

'I can live with it,' she replied.

'But, Claire—'

'Jordan, the day I can't handle a little creep like Peter Thornton is the day I hang up my stethoscope.'

He bit his lip.

'OK,' he said reluctantly, 'but if you ever want help you know that you've only got to ask.'

She nodded, and suddenly a smile curved her lips. 'Do you mean that?'

'Of course I do—we're friends, remember.'

'Any kind of help?'

'I just said so, didn't I?' he said.

'Great.' She beamed. 'Because I need a man for a few minutes.'

His eyes danced. 'That's the best offer I've had all week, but do you think we should? Wouldn't that be well and truly breaking the no-touching rule?'

'Idiot,' she said without rancour. 'I need a man because I've just seen Helen Elliot and her husband getting out of their car.'

He frowned slightly. 'Sorry, but is that supposed to mean something to me?'

'Do you remember me telling you about the patient I had?' she began. 'The one I'd done every test on and yet still couldn't find anything wrong with her?'

'I remember.' He took the ladder from her as she began to carry it to the door. 'You were beginning to wonder whether it might be her husband who had the problem, but as you'd seen him so rarely that you couldn't figure out how you were going to prove it.'

'That was Alan Elliot.'

His frown deepened. 'Well, apart from me breaking into a round of applause, just what, exactly, do you want me to do?'

'Sit in with me when I tell him that I think he's the one with the fertility problem.'

He stared at her for a moment and then a look of deep concern appeared on his face. 'You're worried in case he might react badly to the news, aren't you?'

'If you mean, am I worried that he'll hit me the answer's no. If you mean, am I worried that he'll bolt and never come back the answer's yes.'

'So you want some brawn to make sure that he doesn't bolt?' he observed as he propped the ladder against the wall.

'Got it in one.'

For a few seconds he said nothing and then one corner of his mouth lifted. 'How big is this guy, Claire?'

Her own lips twitched. 'Not *hugely* big.'

'In other words, he's six feet two and built like a tank,' he said, his smile widening.

'Of course he's not,' she exclaimed. 'He can't be any more than…than…'

'Six-one?' he suggested.

A chuckle came from her. 'Something like that. But you've got to be at least six-three.'

'Six-four, to be exact.'

'Well, there you are, then.'

'There I am, what?' he protested.

'You're a good three inches taller than he is.'

'Yes, but I bet he outweighs me by at least three stone!'

She started to laugh and he joined her.

She had such an infectious laugh, he thought. It was the kind of laugh that you remembered—the kind of laugh that seemed to wrap itself around you, warming you. Unconsciously he shook his head. He was straying into dangerous territory again. Friends didn't notice one another's laughter—or if they did it wasn't because it warmed them.

'You don't have to agree, you know,' she continued, misinterpreting that shake of his head. 'If you don't want to do it—'

'And have you think I'm chicken?' he declared. 'OK, I'll sit in with you. But,' he added quickly as she began to thank him, 'before I put myself in the position of having my teeth smashed in, are you absolutely positive that he's the one with the problem?'

She went across to her desk and picked up a file.

'I've done four post-coital tests on Helen, and came up with the same answer every time.'

'How the hell did you manage to persuade her to supply four PCTs?' he gasped.

'Don't ask!' She laughed. 'Look at these results, Jordan. The sperm were hardly moving in any of them.'

He read through the report quickly and sighed. 'We're going to have to deal with this one really carefully, Claire. OK, so four negative PCTs seem pretty conclusive but you know as well as I do that sometimes the results can vary, depending on when you did the tests.'

'Agreed, but statistically it's bound to happen,' she continued doggedly. 'Thirty per cent of all infertility cases are down to the man, and at least there's something we can do about it nowadays. In the past we just had to say we were sorry and that was that.'

He nodded.

'So, will you sit in with me?' she asked.

'Only if you'll let me be the one who tells him what you've found.'

'But he's my patient—'

'He's also a man, Claire,' he interrupted. 'He might accept the news better from me and, even if he doesn't, at least when he's ramming my teeth down my throat I'll feel that I've done something to deserve it.'

She chewed on her lip for a moment and then nodded. 'OK, you can tell him.'

'What about Mrs Elliot?' he asked as he picked up the stepladder again and carried it out into the corridor. 'How do you think she'll react to the news?'

'Knowing Helen, I think she'll refuse to believe it.'

'It's amazing how many women do,' he exclaimed as he followed her along to the store cupboard. 'For some strange reason they seem to prefer the problem to be theirs rather than their husbands'.'

'What's so surprising about that?' she protested. 'Every woman knows what frail little creatures men are.'

'Whoa—put your claws back in!' he said.

'I mean it, Jordan,' she insisted. 'You might not like it, but when it comes to receiving bad news the vast majority of women can take it a whole lot better than men do.'

He opened his mouth and then shook his head ruefully. 'I'm afraid you're right.'

'Of course I am,' she said with a chuckle. 'I'm the boss, aren't I?'

But not for much longer, if Peter Thornton gets his way, Jordan thought with a sinking heart.

'Claire—'

'What will you suggest to the Elliots if they ask you about treatment?' she said.

'If the sperm results continue to be as poor as you've found them they've really only got three choices if they want a baby of their own—IVF, GIFT or AI.'

'And that's something we'll have to discuss later,' Claire replied in an undertone, gazing past him. 'The Elliots have just arrived.'

Jordan glanced in the direction of her gaze and gasped. 'Hell, Claire,' he muttered under his breath. 'The man's built like a wrestler!'

'You were the one who wanted to break the news to him, not me,' she whispered back sweetly.

His blue eyes glinted. 'I'll get even with you for this, Claire Fraser!'

'No chance!' she whispered back as she advanced towards the Elliots with a welcoming smile.

Her smile did not last long. In fact, as soon as Jordan broke the news about the negative PCT tests the atmosphere in the consulting room became so charged that, though she would never have admitted it, she was glad of Jordan's presence.

'I didn't give permission for you to do any tests on me,' Alan Elliot said angrily, his gaze fixed on Claire. 'You had no right to do that!'

'We weren't testing you, Mr Elliot,' she replied quickly, seeing his wife's distress. 'We were only assessing your wife's cervical mucus, and our lab technicians happened to notice that your sperm didn't seem to be moving about very much.'

'Then your lab technicians need their eyes tested,' he flared. 'There's nothing wrong with me.'

'It's certainly possible that the tests were done at the wrong time, Mr Elliot,' Jordan said smoothly. 'Your wife could have ovulated early that month or, indeed, not ovulated at all because she was under stress.'

'Well, there you are,' Alan Elliot declared. 'The tests were wrong.'

'The only way we can know that for certain is if we test you, Alan,' Claire said gently.

'I don't need to be tested,' he insisted. 'My GP examined me and he said I was fine.'

'A physical examination can only tell whether your testes are properly descended,' Jordan observed. 'It can also check for hypospadias—that's a problem with the bladder—and it can pick up a varicocele—a sort of varicose vein—but it can't check on your fertility.'

'If anyone's got the problem it's Helen!' Alan Elliot exclaimed. 'Maybe if she wasn't so damned frigid all the time we'd have a baby by now!'

Helen Elliot turned crimson and a blaze of anger appeared on Jordan's face.

'Mr Elliot, there is absolutely no evidence to suggest that it makes one bit of difference to a woman's fertility if she isn't aroused when making love.'

'Maybe there isn't any concrete evidence, but it sure as hell must make a difference,' he blustered.

'If that were true, perhaps you'd care to explain why women who are raped sometimes become pregnant?' Jordan demanded, his blue eyes ice-cold, his face white. 'I very much doubt if those women experience an orgasm during such a violation.'

'I wouldn't know about that,' Alan retorted. 'All I do know is that maybe if I got a bit of co-operation now and then, instead of feeling that I was trying to make love to a statue, we might have kids by now!'

Jordan half rose in his seat and Claire quickly put her hand on his arm.

'This isn't getting us anywhere,' she said.

'Too right it isn't,' Alan threw back at her. 'I don't have to sit here and listen to some female doctor, who's probably sexually frustrated herself, telling me that I'm not a proper man. Come on, Helen, we're going home!'

He pulled his wife to her feet and made for the door, and Claire groaned inwardly as Jordan followed him.

Alan Elliot might outweigh Jordan by a good three stones but, judging by the furious expression on Jordan's face, she wouldn't have liked to bet money on the outcome if the situation got nasty.

'Look, please don't go,' she begged, also getting to her feet. 'Can't we just all sit down and discuss this matter calmly and rationally?'

'I think I've heard all I want from you, Doctor!' Alan said grimly, and opened the door, only to see Jordan slam it again.

'Mr. Elliot,' Jordan said with some difficulty, 'nobody is questioning your sexual prowess. In fact, you might be interested to know that infertile men often make the best lovers. You're confusing sexuality with fertility, and they're not the same thing.'

Alan Elliot glared at him for a moment and suddenly his huge shoulders sagged. 'Are you sure that I'm the one with the problem?'

'He didn't say that, love,' his wife said quickly. 'He said that the tests they did on me might be wrong. I don't mind if they do them again.'

'And is that what you want, Mr Elliot?' Jordan asked, his eyes fixed on Alan. 'Do you really want your wife to go through all those tests again when a few simple ones on you might tell us what we want to know?'

'You don't have to, Alan,' Helen Elliot exclaimed, her eyes large and dark. 'Like you said, I'm sure there's nothing wrong with you—'

'But how will we know if I don't take the tests?' he murmured unhappily. 'We'll both always wonder—I'll always wonder.' He stared down at his hands for a moment and then squared his jaw. 'OK, Doc. What do you want me to do?'

'I'd like you to provide us with a semen specimen for analysis.'

'You mean right now?' Alan exclaimed, flushing.

'Well, there's no time like the present,' Jordan replied. 'So if you'd like to come with me…?'

With obvious reluctance Alan Elliot followed Jordan out of the door, and as Helen Elliot sat down again Claire smiled encouragingly at her.

'It is for the best, Helen.'

'I suppose so,' she said unhappily, 'but I never thought it might be him.'

'Most couples don't.' Claire sighed.

Helen fidgeted with her bag for a moment and then cleared her throat. 'How…? I mean, the specimen…how does Alan…?'

'Get one?' Claire finished for her. 'Well, we have some

fairly explicit magazines in stock so hopefully your husband shouldn't have too much trouble.'

Helen flushed deeply. 'I see.'

'I'm afraid there's no place for modesty in an infertility clinic,' Claire said gently. 'And it is in a good cause.'

'I know,' Helen replied, 'but I still wish it had been me.'

'It has been you for the last six months,' Claire pointed out. 'Think of all the investigations you've had to put up with, all the intimate examinations.'

'That isn't what I meant, Doctor,' Helen said sadly. 'What I meant was that if we can't have a baby I think Alan could have adjusted to it better if I'd been the one with the problem.'

Well, tough, Claire thought, but she didn't say that. She just nodded as sympathetically as she could.

'What exactly are you looking for in Alan's sample?' Helen asked.

'Basically to see how many sperm there are, and if they're mobile. If the sperm are good they should be swimming in a fairly straight line.'

Helen nodded. 'That Dr Marshall—he's nice, isn't he?'

'Yes—yes, he is,' Claire replied.

In fact, she thought with a deep sigh, he was very nice indeed.

Let's just be friends, he had said, and she was trying so hard to regard him as just that, but surely your heart shouldn't flip over when a friend smiled at you? Surely there shouldn't be an aching warmth deep in the pit of your stomach if he was near?

She sighed again. And this was the man she'd invited to spend Christmas Day with her. She must have been out of her mind.

'Doctor—'

'Ah, here's your husband,' Claire said with relief as Alan and Jordan came back into the room.

'If—and I'm only saying *if*—there's a problem with me,'

Alan Elliot declared as he sat down again, 'what could have caused it?'

'Mumps can affect your fertility,' Jordan observed.

'Never had them.'

'A prostate infection—'

'Never had one of those either.'

'I'm afraid male infertility is one of the most complicated areas of medicine, Alan,' Jordan said ruefully. 'What can lower one man's sperm count has absolutely no effect on someone else's. It all depends on your predisposition.'

Alan Elliot frowned and shook his head. 'I'm sorry, but I don't follow.'

'What I mean is that if your sperm count's low to start with, it doesn't really take much to knock it for six. Smoking can affect it so can excessive drinking and being overweight.'

'In other words, you want to turn me into a fitness freak,' Alan complained.

'Strangely enough, that's the very last thing I'd recommend.' Jordan laughed. 'Excessive exercise can actually be very bad for your sperm count.'

'When…when do you think you'll get my results?' Alan asked.

'With it being Christmas next week, it will probably take a little longer than usual so if you could come back to us on…' Jordan looked at Claire enquiringly and she handed him her appointment book. 'On the fourteenth of January—'

'You can't see us until then?' Alan gasped.

'I'm sorry but we can't. Look, try and forget about it and just enjoy Christmas,' Jordan continued as Alan looked distinctly crestfallen. 'I know it won't be easy, but this is just your first test—there will be lots more before we can say anything with absolute certainty.'

'I guess so,' Alan Elliot muttered without conviction as he and his wife went out of the door.

'That was tough,' Claire exclaimed as soon as the Elliots

had gone. 'I thought at one point that you were going to hit him.'

'Nonsense,' Jordan replied lightly. 'I told you before that I never lose my temper.'

She gazed at him for a moment and cleared her throat awkwardly. 'Is that because you're afraid that if you ever really did let yourself go you'd hurt someone, as your father did?'

His head shot around to her.

'You missed your vocation, Claire,' he said tightly. 'You should have been a psychiatrist or a social worker.'

'Are you afraid of that?' she pressed.

For a moment he said nothing and then he sighed. 'When you've grown up in a household as violent as mine was, you can't help but wonder. I used to drive Sophy mad the way I would never argue with her, but I was always afraid... Afraid that one day I'd lose control and become like my father.'

'I'd say that was pretty unlikely,' she said encouragingly. 'You know the dangers, and knowing them is half the battle.'

'I suppose so,' he murmured, and shook his head at her with a smile. 'I'm damned if I know how you do it, Claire Fraser, but you seem to have this knack of getting me to talk about myself.'

'Maybe you should have done it a long time ago,' she replied, only to see him shake his head again.

'Old habits die hard, Claire. I learned when I was very young to keep my thoughts and my feelings to myself unless I wanted to be battered from here to kingdom come.'

'But you don't have to do that now,' she said gently. 'You can move on—change.'

His lips curved. 'Is that an order?'

'Just a bit of advice from a friend, that's all,' she replied quietly.

He gazed at her for a moment and his face grew suddenly serious. 'Will you take some advice from a friend, Claire?'

'It depends upon what it is,' she laughed.

He knew that he had to put a spoke in Peter Thornton's wheel somehow and there was only one way that he could do it.

'It's about the clinic,' he began slowly. 'You're running it very well, but with my help you could make it the best-run department in the hospital.'

The laughter disappeared from her face in an instant.

'You're saying I can't cope,' she said, her voice cold.

'No, I'm not saying that,' he declared, 'but you've been looking so tired lately—'

'Roz is tired, the lab technicians are tired and the clinic's nurses are tired,' she interjected, her jaw tight. 'If you want to play good Samaritan, go and help them.'

'I can't—I don't have the expertise—but I can help you,' he said. 'Claire, I've run my own department. I know the pressures, but I also know the short cuts that could lighten your workload.'

'No.'

'You and I could work out a new schedule together. I'm sure the clinic nurses could take on some of the simpler cases—they're certainly qualified enough—and I could do some of your paperwork and take on more patients—'

'No.'

'Claire, at the moment you're running yourself into the ground, rushing round trying to catch your tail—'

'Jordan, who's the head of department here?'

'Claire—'

'Who's the head of department?' she demanded.

'You are.'

'That's right.' She nodded. 'I am. I make the decisions, I work out the schedules and I allocate the patients.'

'But if you would only let me help you—'

'How many times do I have to say no?' she said angrily. 'I don't want your help—I don't want anybody's help.'

'But—'

'Jordan, when I got promotion at the Rochester clinic

everyone said it was because I was Max's wife. When I got the assistant head of department's job here everyone said it was because I was Max's ex-wife. Now I'm head of the department and I want to show that I can do it on my own.'

'But, Claire—'

'No, Jordan.' She swept out of her room.

For a moment he didn't move and then he went after her. 'Claire!'

She turned in the centre of the corridor, her grey eyes stormy.

'I was only trying to help,' he said gently.

For a moment she gazed back at him and then she smiled with difficulty. 'I know, and I appreciate it, but I have to do this on my own, Jordan. Whether I sink or swim, I have to do this on my own.'

And it looked very much as though she was going to sink if Peter Thornton had his way, he thought with a deep sigh.

'OK, Claire,' he declared, 'but if you ever need any help—'

'I'll ask for it.'

He smiled ruefully. 'I doubt it.'

'Of course I will,' she said, 'because that's what friends are for, aren't they? To help you when times get rough?'

His smile became oddly twisted.

'Yes, Claire,' he said. 'That's what friends are for.'

CHAPTER SIX

'ALL I can say is thank God it's Christmas Eve,' Anne Sommerville declared as she accompanied Claire up the stairs. 'If I didn't have this holiday to look forward to, I think I'd run away.'

Claire sighed. 'I know what you mean. I knew being head of a department wasn't going to be easy but I've got to admit that it's a whole lot tougher than I ever thought.'

'If you're really finding it difficult, why don't you ask Jordan for help?' Anne observed. 'He's run his own department, hasn't he?'

Claire came to a halt and eyed her suspiciously. 'Has he been talking to you?'

'Of course he hasn't—why should he?'

'Because he never stops offering me help, that's why.'

'Then grab it with both hands,' Anne said. 'I would.'

'Would you?' Claire exclaimed in surprise.

'Of course,' Anne chuckled. 'Being independent's one thing—being a martyr's something else.'

'I'm not being a martyr,' Claire protested. 'I just want to prove that I can run the department on my own.'

'I don't see how taking a bit of advice from someone with his experience means you've failed,' Anne observed. 'In fact, I'd say that it showed you were sensible enough to want to learn from someone else's mistakes.'

'I suppose so,' Claire said with a slight frown as she began to walk up the stairs again.

'Talking about learning,' Anne continued, her brown eyes sparkling, 'what's this I hear about you spending Christmas with Jordan?'

Claire came to a halt. 'Who told you that?'

'Well, I just happened to meet Jordan in the corridor, and I just happened to ask him what he was doing for Christmas, and—'

'And he just happened to say he was spending it with me,' Claire finished for her. 'Well, he isn't spending it with me—he's just coming for lunch.'

'Same difference,' Anne said dismissively. 'So tell me everything—and don't leave out any of the juicy details. When did the two of you get together?'

Claire shook her head and laughed, irritatedly aware that she was blushing. 'We haven't got together. Jordan and I are just friends, that's all.'

'Oh, really?' Anne exclaimed, her eyebrows rising.

'Yes, really,' Claire said firmly. 'And I don't want to hear any whispers to the contrary, going round the hospital, Dr Sommerville.'

'As if I would,' Anne protested.

'You know very well that you would.' Claire chuckled. 'Jordan and I are just friends. That's what he wants, and that's what I want.'

'But, Claire—'

'Lord, is that the time?' she said as she glanced down at her watch. 'I've got to run.'

'But—'

Claire didn't wait for her to say any more. She just waved her hand and flew up the remaining stairs into the safety of her own department.

'Where's the fire?' Roz exclaimed when Claire appeared breathlessly at her office door.

'No fire—I'm just escaping from somebody,' she replied.

Roz's lips twitched. 'Sybil from the lab or Dr Sommerville?'

'Dr Sommerville,' Claire said wryly.

Roz's smile widened. 'Let me guess—she wanted to know how come you were spending Christmas with Jordan?'

Claire rolled her eyes heavenwards. 'This has got to be

one of the worst-kept secrets in the hospital. Who told you?'

'A little bird.'

'This little bird wouldn't happen to be six feet four with blond hair and blue eyes, would it?' Claire demanded, and saw Roz laugh.

'Be fair, Claire. He had to tell someone where he was spending Christmas in case the hospital needed to contact him.'

'He is not spending Christmas with me,' Claire declared slowly and deliberately. 'He is only coming for lunch. And that is absolutely and categorically my last word on the subject,' she added as Roz opened her mouth, clearly dying to know more. 'Got it?'

Roz expressively drew her finger along her throat. 'Got it.'

'Then perhaps we might get down to something more important,' Claire said. 'The lab said that they sent up Alan Elliot's sperm test results this morning—'

'They did. Jordan's got them.'

'Jordan?' Claire said in surprise.

'He asked if he could take a look at them so I gave them to him. That was all right, wasn't it?' Roz added, as a slight frown appeared on Claire's forehead. 'He said he'd sat in with you when you saw Mr Elliot—'

'It's OK, Roz.'

But it wasn't OK, Claire thought with a niggle of irritation as she made her way down to Jordan's room. Alan Elliot was her patient and she should have seen the results first. OK, so Jordan had been really helpful when they'd seen Alan, but being helpful was one thing and commandeering her patient was something else.

'Hi, there.' Jordan smiled as she opened his door. 'Something I can help you with?'

'Roz said you had Alan Elliot's sperm results,' she said. He reached into his desk and pulled them out.

'Actually, I've been meaning to speak to you about him,'

he said awkwardly as she held out her hand for them. 'Alan has asked if he and his wife could be transferred to my list. Apparently he would feel more comfortable with a male doctor.'

Her hand fell to her side. 'I see.'

'It's not a reflection on your ability or anything,' he said as she stared at him impassively. 'It's just—'

'He would feel more comfortable with a male doctor,' she finished for him. 'I understand.'

And she did, but that didn't mean she had to like it. She'd worked hard with Helen Elliot over the past few months and for her to change doctors now, just when they might be getting somewhere, was frustrating in the extreme.

'May I see the results the lab got from the swim-up and velocity tests you did on Alan Elliot?' she asked, trying— and failing—to keep the irritation out of her voice.

He gazed up at her. 'Look, if you'd rather Alan stayed with you, I could have a word with him—'

'And have him think that he's being pressurised into not changing doctors?' She shook her head. 'If he would prefer to see you I can live with it.'

And she could. It was just distinctly disconcerting to realise that in the short time Jordan had been at the clinic three other sets of patients had asked to change to him, too.

'It isn't a personal criticism, Claire,' he said gently, as though he'd read her mind. 'It's just that sometimes patients take more to one doctor than another.'

He was right—she knew he was.

God, but she really must be tired, she thought as she managed to nod and smile back at him. If she didn't watch out she could see herself starting to wonder if he was actively poaching patients from her.

'There were some sperm in the samples we took,' he continued as he spread the results out on the desk in front of her, 'so the tubes from the testes to the seminal vesicles aren't blocked and the muscles that pump semen through the penis are working properly.'

'Thank goodness for that,' Claire said, as she leant over the desk to take a closer look. 'I wouldn't have liked to have been the one to tell him that his testes weren't producing any sperm. It's virtually impossible to treat.'

'It looks as though his sperm are just of poor quality. Some of them were moving in a reasonably straight line but not a lot.'

'What was the volume of ejaculate?'

'I've got the report here somewhere,' he replied, riffling through papers on his desk.

'Here—here it is,' she exclaimed, reaching for the piece of paper just as he did.

His hand brushed hers and she pulled away as if she'd been stung.

'Sorry,' he murmured, without lifting his head.

'N-no problem,' she stammered, feeling her heart contract.

'Nought point six millilitres.'

'What?' she asked in confusion.

His blue eyes met hers. 'The volume of Alan Elliot's ejaculate—it was 0.6 millilitres.'

'Good,' she declared, bending quickly over the report again. 'There doesn't seem to be any sign of inflammation in his glands, then?'

'No.'

'Good,' she repeated, trying not to notice that Jordan's chest seemed to be rising and falling as rapidly as her own heartbeat.

'I see you tested Mrs Elliot's cervix to see if she was producing antibodies to the sperm?' he observed.

She nodded. 'It was a bit of a long shot, but I thought I'd better check it out.'

'It's always wise to cover every eventuality.'

She nodded again, and wished with all her heart that she could just as easily cover every eventuality with him. Why, oh why, she wondered, was this friendship thing so hard to do?

She knew the dangers of allowing anything else to develop between them, and every night when she went home she told herself that tomorrow would be different—tomorrow she would have her feelings under control. But she only had to catch a glimpse of his blond head at the end of the corridor to know that her feelings were anything but under control.

'Are you going to suggest hormone treatment?' she asked, keeping her eyes fixed on the report with all the appearance of being engrossed. 'Sometimes if you give large doses of testosterone for a short period you get a rebound effect and the sperm become temporarily stronger.'

'I think he's really only got two viable choices—AI or ICSI.'

She edged casually away from the desk and forced herself to meet his gaze.

'I wouldn't recommend artificial insemination. I know it can work,' she continued as his eyebrows rose questioningly, 'but the process is so clinical. It puts a tremendous strain on any couple's love life.'

'I know.' He sighed. 'Precise timing of ovulation is essential, and then if the man can't masturbate to order it can be very embarrassing for him.'

'ICSI, then?'

'I think so. Even with poor sperm, fertilisation usually occurs in between twenty-five and thirty per cent of cases after an intracystoplasmic sperm injection.'

'It'll mean that Helen will have to go through the whole IVF course, even though there's nothing wrong with her,' Claire observed.

'It's the only way we can be sure of collecting the eggs, and I don't think she'll mind, do you?'

She shook her head and watched him gather up the pieces of paper on his desk.

'Something else I can do for you?' he asked, glancing up as he sensed her gaze on him.

Oh, yes, her mind whispered as she felt a dull, throbbing

ache between her legs. There's definitely something you can do for me. Stop it Claire, she told herself, stop it.

'Mr Kennedy has asked if some of his gynae students can watch one of our ops,' she replied, fighting down her mounting colour. 'I've a cornual anastomosis coming up but, frankly, I hate an audience and I wondered if you'd like to do it?'

'When is it?' he asked, reaching for his appointment book.

'Not until the sixteenth of February but, knowing how busy we both are, I thought I'd give you plenty of warning.'

He flicked through his book and nodded. 'I can do it, no problem. Are you busy right now?' he continued as she turned to go.

'Only paperwork,' she answered. 'Why?'

'The Hardings start their IVF treatment today and I wondered if you'd like to sit in when I see them?'

'But they're your patients now,' she said, bewildered.

'They were yours first,' he observed, 'and I know how unhappy you are about them opting for IVF.'

'What I think isn't important,' she pointed out. 'They're not my patients any more.'

'No, but you've known them a lot longer than I have, and...'

'And?' she prompted, as a smile tugged at his lips.

'If it works you'll have to concede that I was right, and if it doesn't you can have the satisfaction of saying, "I told you so".'

An answering smile slowly crept to her lips and she sighed inwardly. Why, oh, why, did she have to like him so much? If only she didn't like him so much there wouldn't be any problem.

'OK,' she said, outwardly calm. 'Just so long as you understand that if you say or do anything that I disapprove of I'll say so.'

'So what else is new?' he grinned.

*   *   *

That Liz Harding was both excited and nervous at the prospect of starting her IVF treatment was obvious. She sat on the edge of her seat, clasping and unclasping her hands, until eventually Claire shook her head at her.

'This isn't the dentist's, you know, Liz.'

'I know, I know.' She laughed. 'But I've been thinking about today for so long, and now it's actually arrived…'

'You're happy and terrified at the same time?' Claire suggested.

Liz nodded tremulously. 'I just so want it to work.'

Every infertile woman did, Claire thought with an inward sigh.

'Dr Marshall will have explained that he's going to start you on some gonadotrophin-releasing hormone this morning,' she said instead.

Liz nodded again. 'It's supposed to suppress my pituitary gland, isn't it, so that you can have a greater control over any eggs I might produce?'

'That's right,' Claire replied. 'The drug comes in a nasal spray so it's not difficult to use, but you must keep on using it until we tell you to stop.'

'Just be careful about how and where you use it, Liz,' Jordan observed, his lips crinkling. 'We've had patients whose families thought they'd suddenly started to sniff cocaine.'

Liz laughed and her husband did, too.

Oh, he was good, Claire thought as she watched the Hardings relax. In fact, he was pretty much the perfect consultant, and as a man…

She groaned inwardly. What was she doing?

She was letting her body rule her head, that's what she was doing. Think of Max, she told herself. Remember how miserable and unhappy you made him. Remember how wretched you felt when he found someone else.

'There's one thing I ought to warn you about,' Jordan continued as he handed Liz her nasal spray. 'Because the GnRH will suppress your pituitary gland, you might get hot flushes and headaches and generally feel quite depressed while you're using it.'

'Are you trying to put me off, Doctor?' Liz chuckled and Jordan smiled.

'Just being realistic. I'm hoping you won't feel too uncomfortable, but if you do feel weak or faint, or notice any reduction in your urine, please contact us right away—your ovaries could be overstimulating.'

Liz nodded. 'My period should start a few days after I start this GnRH, shouldn't it?'

'That's right,' Claire replied, as Jordan glanced across at her, clearly expecting her to answer. 'Phone the unit as soon as they start so that we can give you an ultrasound scan, and then start you on your daily injections of Pergonal.'

'The Pergonal stimulates follicular growth in the ovary, doesn't it?' Bob Harding observed.

Claire nodded. 'The average number of injections is usually around fourteen, but Liz could need more or she could need less.'

'And what happens when you think Liz has produced enough follicles?' Bob asked.

'It's not a question of *when*, Bob, but *if*,' Jordan said gently. 'There's no guarantee that Liz will produce any follicles at all.'

'But if she does,' Bob pressed.

'If she does, then that's when we give her a final injection of human chorionic gonadotrophin. We usually administer it about thirty-six hours before we collect the eggs so that the eggs are mature but still in the ovary.'

'And then Liz goes to the theatre?' Bob said.

'Then she goes to the theatre,' Jordan confirmed. 'The eggs are collected, by inserting a fine needle into the vagina, and Liz can opt for either a local or a general anaesthetic.'

Liz grimaced. 'I think I'd prefer to be totally unconscious, if you don't mind.'

'Most women do,' Jordan said with a smile. 'And it's at

this point that we'll need a fresh sample of sperm from you, Bob.'

'I was wondering when we'd get to my bit.' He grinned.

'If the sperm are healthy we'll add a small number to each egg in a culture dish,' Jordan explained. 'Hopefully, some of them will start to grow into embryos, and if they do we'll leave them for about a day to check that they are developing normally.'

'And then the eggs go back inside me?' Liz asked.

'*If* they're fertilised,' Jordan cautioned. 'I have to emphasise that fertilisation might not take place even if a good number of eggs have been collected and the sperm seem fine and healthy.'

'But if they are fertilised?' Liz said.

'Then we'll put up to three embryos into your uterus via a very fine catheter,' Jordan replied.

'And that's it?' Bob said.

Jordan glanced across at Claire and she smiled wryly.

'I'm afraid this is when the waiting really starts,' she said. 'If the treatment has been successful, one or more of the embryos might implant in the lining of the womb and for each of them a foetus and placenta might develop.'

'How long do we have to wait until we know whether that's happened?' Liz asked.

'We'll take occasional blood samples from you for about twelve days and then we'll take a urine test to see if you're pregnant,' Claire answered.

Liz smiled at her. 'I will be—I just know I will be.'

Claire said nothing as the couple got up to leave. Only time would tell if Liz's optimism was well founded and the last thing Claire wanted was to dampen her spirits.

'I think you might have been right about the Hardings, not being up to IVF just yet,' Jordan said with a frown as soon as he and Claire were alone. 'Liz seems convinced that it's going to work first time and statistically the odds are pretty much against that happening.'

'She might be lucky,' Claire replied as she watched him

hang up his white coat. 'All we can do is wait and hope. And now I must go—I've a couple coming in for their first consultation.'

'At five o'clock on Christmas Eve?' he protested.

'I know, I know,' she said ruefully, as he shook his head at her, 'but they've been waiting for an appointment to see me for two years, Jordan.'

He sighed. 'You're running yourself into the ground—you know that, don't you? Why won't you let me help you?'

For a second she was tempted. Maybe Anne was right. Maybe she was just being foolish, but she couldn't forget all those sly little innuendos that she'd overheard when she'd been appointed head of department. The innuendos that suggested she'd only been appointed because of whom she knew.

'You didn't talk me round last time, Jordan,' she said firmly, 'and you're not going to do it now.'

'It was worth a try, though, wasn't it?' he said as she followed him out of his room. 'And now I've got to go myself. I've got some last-minute Christmas shopping to do.'

'It's easy to see you've never shopped in Glasgow on Christmas Eve before,' she observed. 'You'll get squashed in Byres Road, flattened in Sauchiehall Street and trampled to death in Argyle Street.'

'I'll risk it,' he said. 'Which reminds me—what time do you want me to come tomorrow?'

The smile on her face became fixed. It had sounded so easy when he had first suggested that they share their Christmas lunch but suddenly she knew that she couldn't do it. She just couldn't spend a whole afternoon alone with him in her flat.

'Jordan, about tomorrow—'

'Around half eleven be OK?'

'Jordan—'

'I'm really looking forward to it, Claire,' he smiled. 'Eating too much, probably drinking a bit too much and then sitting slumped in front of the TV.'

Tell him that he can't come, a voice in her mind urged. Tell him that you don't want to do it any more.

'Jordan—'

'Actually, the truth is that since Sophy left Christmases have been pretty wretched occasions for me,' he continued awkwardly, 'and it will be wonderful to be able to share it with someone again.'

She gazed at him for a moment, her mind a whirl of conflicting emotions, and then cleared her throat. 'Around half past eleven will be fine.'

But at a quarter past eleven the next morning she had decided that it was anything but fine.

'Oh, for God's sake, make up your mind,' she told herself as she flicked desperately through her wardrobe for the tenth time. 'Jordan's going to be here any minute, and if you don't choose something soon he'll find you in your underwear!'

With a muttered oath she hauled out a wide tartan skirt and a cream blouse, which she'd had for years, and put them on. What did it matter what she wore, anyway? Friends didn't dress up to impress friends.

Defiantly she brushed her hair back into a high ponytail and surveyed herself without enthusiasm. Maybe her hair might be better down. Maybe she should wear a dress. She opened her wardrobe door again and groaned as her door-bell rang.

It was too late to change, too late to do anything, and with a belligerent frown she went along the hall and opened the door, only to stare in amazement at the seven-foot Christmas tree, standing on her doorstep.

'Jordan?' she said uncertainly.

'Merry Christmas!' he exclaimed, popping his head through the branches. 'Not too early, am I?'

'N-no,' she stammered as he dragged in the tree and then

followed it up with two large boxes. 'Jordan, are you coming for lunch or moving in?'

He grinned. 'Is that a proposition?'

She shook her head at him severely. 'What's in the boxes?'

'The chicken, the pâté, a trifle and some wine in this one,' he replied, carrying one of the boxes through to the kitchen. 'The other one's got the Christmas tree lights and decorations in it. What do you think of our tree, by the way?' he continued as he went back to the front door and lifted it up.

'It's…it's lovely,' she murmured, 'but I'm afraid I've already got one.'

His face fell. 'Real or artificial?'

'Artificial.'

'Then you haven't got a tree,' he declared. 'Not like this.'

'You can say that again,' she observed, her lips twitching as the top of the tree caught the hallway light and sent it swinging.

He laughed, and she did, too, but when their laughter died they were left staring awkwardly at each other.

It's going to be a nightmare, she thought with a sinking heart. It's going to be a complete and utter nightmare. How could they get through six hours of each other's company if they couldn't even manage six minutes, without feeling ill at ease?

'Would you like a coffee…a drink?' she said in desperation.

He shook his head. 'I'd better get this tree up.'

She nodded but he didn't move. He just stood there, staring down at her, until her hand crept uncomfortably to the neck of her blouse.

'Is there something wrong?' she asked.

'I was just thinking how very lovely you look,' he said, before he turned abruptly on his heel and walked off down the hall, dragging the tree behind him.

For a second she stared after him and then headed for the kitchen, her brain working overtime.

An hour, she thought. It ought to take him at least an hour to put up and decorate the tree. Then they could have lunch and watch the afternoon movie on TV. That should take them safely to teatime and then, she thought with a sigh of relief, he would go.

'The tree's finished,' he said right on cue almost an hour later.

'And our lunch is ready,' she replied. 'So, what do you want to do first—eat or have me admire your handiwork?'

'Eat, of course,' he grinned. 'I'm starving.'

And he was. He ate everything she put in front of him, and she knew that if it had been anyone else but him, sitting opposite her, she would have considered herself lucky to have such an amusing and entertaining guest. But it wasn't anyone else. It was Jordan Marshall and she was only too acutely aware of it.

Stop it, her little voice whispered as she found her eyes constantly straying to the gentle curve of his lips as he told her about the places he'd visited in America. Pull yourself together, she urged as her body tensed whenever he stretched across her for the wine. But he's so attractive, her heart sighed, so very attractive.

And you're a fool, she told herself. You've been this way once—haven't you learned anything from the past?

'Let's take a look at this wonderful tree of yours, then,' she said when he finally pushed his empty coffee-cup away and leant back in his seat with a sigh of contentment.

'Don't I get a rest first after a wonderful meal like that?' he protested.

'Later—you can rest later,' she said, getting to her feet, knowing that she had to move even if it was only into the sitting room.

Grumbling, he followed her along the hall.

'Well, what do you think?' he asked as she opened the sitting-room door.

She gasped. 'Jordan, it's…it's beautiful.'

And it was. The glittering tinsel, the lights, softly glowing amongst the pine needles, and the shimmering decorations were a work of art.

'Hey, what did you expect?' He grinned. 'Surgeons are supposed to have good hands.'

'They weren't much in evidence when you were carving the chicken,' she declared with a chuckle. 'That poor bird looks as though it's been attacked by a chainsaw.'

'People and trees—that's my speciality,' he exclaimed, and then dived behind the tree to produce a small package. 'I got something for you. It's not much, but it is Christmas…'

She went across to her desk.

'Snap!' she said as she took out a parcel.

She had never intended to buy him anything—in fact, she had been quite determined that she wouldn't. But last night, as she'd stood in the centre of Byres Road, surrounded by frantic Christmas shoppers, she'd told herself that it would be deeply embarrassing if he had bought her something and she had nothing to give him in return.

That's what she'd told herself but as she anxiously watched him, unwrapping her gift, she knew only too well that something else had prompted her actions.

'If they don't fit, or they're not really what you want, I can take them back,' she said, as he stared down at the pair of biking gloves she had bought him.

'They're wonderful,' he said softly. 'In fact, they're the best present anyone has ever given me.'

'Well, they're useful anyway,' she said briskly, unaccountably moved by his obvious pleasure.

'Your turn now,' he said.

Quickly she unwrapped his present, to find that he had bought her three pairs of the most expensive stockings on the market.

'I didn't know what to get,' he said, 'but I thought, well, I thought great legs deserve great stockings.'

She blushed and shook her head. 'Flattery will get you nowhere, Jordan Marshall.'

'Merry Christmas, Claire.'

His voice was unexpectedly husky, and she looked up to find his eyes fixed on her, eyes that were warm and tender. No, Claire, she told herself as her heart began to drum against her ribcage. No, no, no.

She took a step back, only to find herself jammed up against her desk, and when he reached out and cupped her face gently in his hands she stiffened.

He was going to kiss her, she knew he was, but it would be all right, she told herself. It would simply be a kiss between friends, but as soon as his lips touched hers she knew that she'd been wrong.

Every nerve in her body responded to the insistent demands of his mouth. Every part of her quivered with a desperate longing as his hands drew her closer to him.

This is wrong, her mind whispered as his fingers eased her blouse free from her skirt. You're going to regret this, her heart sighed as a throbbing heat began to spread throughout her as his hands slid slowly upwards, searching and then finding the catch on her bra.

'Claire…oh, Claire,' he whispered hoarsely into her neck.

She closed her eyes, biting on her lips to stifle a groan as his fingers curled around her already erect nipples and wave upon wave of dizzying sensation assailed her. She dug her fingers deep into his shoulders as his hands cupped her hard against him, and then suddenly she remembered Max. She remembered how much she had once loved him and how much he had once loved her, and she jerked herself out of his arms with a muffled cry of dismay.

'Claire—'

'No,' she said, pulling the two sides of her blouse together with a trembling hand.

'But, Claire—'

'I think…I think you'd better go,' she said, her breathing erratic.

He gazed at her for a moment and then shook his head. 'I know, but the trouble is I don't want to.'

'Jordan, what just happened—it was as much my fault as it was yours, and I admit it,' she said unsteadily. 'But we've just broken every rule of the friendship charter.'

'To hell with the friendship charter!' he exclaimed.

She gazed at him in bewilderment. 'But you don't want to get involved with me any more than I want to get involved with you.'

'Don't I?'

His eyes were fixed on her and she felt the familiar catapulting of her heart.

'You know you don't,' she floundered. 'You said yourself that you were impossible to live with.'

'So I'll change.'

'Jordan, be sensible,' she cried. 'I'm committed to my work, you're committed to your work—'

'Then we'll bore one another rigid, instead of making two other people unhappy.'

'Jordan—'

'Claire, I think…I think I'm falling in love with you,' he said, and as soon as the words were out of his mouth he knew that they were true.

She shook her head at him. 'You can't. I won't allow you to.'

A wry smile appeared on his lips. 'You may be my boss, Claire, but that's one order you can't give me.'

'Jordan, it won't work,' she said desperately.

'We can make it work,' he insisted. 'We both know the dangers—'

'Which is why you said we should just stay friends,' she exclaimed.

'But I don't want to be just friends with you,' he said huskily. 'I want more—I want you.'

She wrapped her arms tightly around herself. She wanted

him, too, she knew she did, but she didn't want the heart-break that she knew would surely follow.

'I'm sorry, Jordan, but I can't.'

'Claire—'

'No,' she whispered, her grey eyes strained and dark. 'I'm sorry—I truly am sorry—but I just can't.'

For once in her life her face couldn't have been inscrutable because he sighed.

'OK, my lovely,' he said softly.

'So...so what happens now?' she said, her voice constricted.

He scratched the back of his neck awkwardly. 'I don't know, Claire, I—' Suddenly a smile curved his lips, a smile that grew and widened. 'Yes, I do know. I'm going to woo you.'

She stared at him, stunned. 'You're going to do what?'

'Woo you, court you.'

She laughed shakily. 'Nobody does that any more, Jordan.'

'Then I'll start a new trend. I'm going to buy you flowers, Claire. I'm going to ask you out on dates and take you home in the evening, without even giving you so much as a chaste kiss on your cheek. I'm going to lay siege to your heart, Claire Fraser, until you say yes.'

'Jordan, don't, please, don't,' she said. 'I'm not worth it.'

'Oh, yes, you are,' he said, reaching out to trace the outline of her jaw with his finger. 'To me you are worth any price.'

A hard lump seemed wedged in her throat and she swallowed it with difficulty. 'Jordan—'

'And now I really had better go,' he said firmly. 'You need to think and I...' He smiled ruefully. 'Right now, I could do with a long cold shower.'

'Jordan, this isn't going to work,' she protested as she followed him down the hall. 'You're making a mistake.'

He opened the front door and shook his head. 'My mistake was thinking we could just be friends.'

It had been her mistake, too, she thought as she watched him walk away. They couldn't just be friends, but they couldn't be anything else either. Not if they didn't want to end up hurting each other badly.

CHAPTER SEVEN

'GOOD grief, Claire, I thought you said Mr Kennedy was just sending along a few of his students to watch this op,' Jordan protested as he peered through the door of the operating theatre. 'It looks like a royal command performance out there!'

Claire shook her head and laughed. 'Just as well you're not operating on a chicken, then.'

'Oh, very funny,' he said with a grin as he pulled up his mask. 'OK, let's get out there and entertain the masses.'

'Masses' was the right word, Claire thought as she followed him into the operating theatre. She'd fully expected all of John Kennedy's students to turn up because it wasn't every day that you got to watch a cornual anastomosis, but what she hadn't expected was to see the observation gallery quite so full—and full of the unlikeliest of people.

It wasn't hard to guess why so many nurses had turned up. Their interest was plainly centred on the man who was performing the operation rather than the operation itself, but what she couldn't understand was why Peter Thornton and three members of the hospital board were there.

She glanced quickly across at Jordan and saw that he, too, had noticed the quartet's presence, but if she was puzzled by it he seemed downright furious.

'Is Mrs Thompson out yet, Bill?' he demanded more curtly than she had ever heard him.

The anaesthetist blinked. 'Of course.'

'Keep an eye on her BP and cardiac output and let me know immediately if there's any change,' Jordan continued.

'I always do,' Bill Morton replied mildly, and raised his eyebrows in puzzled enquiry at Claire.

Casually she edged across to Jordan.

'Are you OK?' she asked in an undertone.

For a second the frown lines on his forehead deepened and then his eyes smiled. 'Never better, my lovely.'

She let out the breath she had been unconsciously holding. For one awful moment she'd thought he'd frozen at the thought of performing an operation in front of such a large audience, but as he flexed his fingers and made his first swift incision she realised she had been wrong. Whatever had momentarily thrown him, it hadn't been the presence of the crowd.

"As Dr Fraser will already have explained, our patient suffers from tubal blockage,' Jordan said as Mr Kennedy's students clustered around the screen that had been erected to show the operation in detail. 'The blockage has occurred where the tube joins the uterus at its narrowest part.'

He straightened momentarily. 'Does anyone have any idea why this blockage might have occurred?'

A ripple of whispered comment ran round the students and a hand went up.

'It could happen after an infection with a coil, sir, or following pregnancy or a miscarriage.'

'That's right—but I'm not a Sir, not yet, anyway,' Jordan replied, and the students laughed. 'Sister Carlton—microscope, please.'

'How does it look?' Claire asked, after he had manipulated the microscope and tiny instruments into Mrs Thompson's abdomen.

'The lining isn't too damaged,' he replied, 'and I think I've got enough Fallopian tube to work with. Want to see?'

She did.

'There's not a whole lot of Fallopian tube.' She frowned as she stared down the microscope.

'Enough.'

Maybe there was for him, but she wouldn't have liked to have tackled it with quite so many people breathing down her neck.

'Ready to go?' she asked.

He shot her a warm smile and nodded, but that was the last smile she exchanged with him once he began to operate in earnest.

Aided only by a microscope and the tiniest of instruments, Jordan was attempting not only to cut out the blocked section of the Fallopian tube but also to stitch the remainder back onto the original opening. As the internal diameter of the tube was less than the thickness of a piece of thread he needed a steady hand, a perfect eye and absolute concentration.

'He's good, isn't he?' Debbie Carlton murmured as she watched him.

Claire nodded. That was the understatement of the year. The man was brilliant.

'Would you close for me, Dr Fraser?' he said at last, easing his shoulders before going over to the students to see if they had any questions.

Quickly Claire took his place. Out of the corner of her eye she could see that Peter and the three members of the board were leaving, and for a second a slight frown appeared on her forehead. Neither he nor any of the board had ever come to see one of their operations before, but maybe it was a good sign. Maybe it meant that Peter was finally starting to take her department seriously.

'Nice work, Jordan,' she said when he finally joined her in the changing room.

He pulled off his cap and mask and grinned. 'I think the audience got their money's worth.'

'You had me a bit worried at the beginning,' she commented, as she ran some water into the sink.

'Initial incision too small, you mean?'

She shook her head. 'Snapping off Bill Morton's head the way you did.'

'Did I?'

'You know you did,' she protested.

'Couldn't have been me,' he said, as he dragged his operating top over his head. 'Must have been some other bloke.'

Quickly she turned her back on him and busied herself, washing her hands. Why did he have to do that? Just when she'd thought she'd got her emotions under control he had to do something like that and her knees instantly seemed to turn to jelly.

'Sounded like you—looked like you,' she said lightly. 'I wondered if maybe you were nervous?'

A pair of firm hands slid round her waist. 'This is the only body that's ever got me nervous.'

'Jordan, don't!' she exclaimed, trying to wriggle free as somewhere deep inside her stomach a warm, sweet shiver stirred.

His hold tightened and his lips curved. 'Why not?'

'Because I don't like it,' she said, flustered.

One eyebrow rose. 'No? Now, I wonder what else you don't like?'

'Stop it, Jordan,' she protested as he began to nuzzle the back of her neck. 'You said you were going to woo me, court me—'

'Which is exactly what I've been doing for the last six weeks,' he replied. 'I've sent you flowers—'

'Yes, but you sent so many that Mrs Wright from number 20 offered me her condolences.'

'And I've taken you to all those God-awful Harrison Ford films because you said he was your favourite.'

'You said you liked him, too,' she declared, trying to pull herself free without success.

'I lied,' he murmured, and nibbled her ear, only to hear her giggle. 'Why, Claire, you're ticklish!'

'No, I'm not,' she said, only to let out another chuckle that totally belied her words. 'Jordan, if you don't stop this right now I swear I'll make you sorry!'

'Promises, promises,' he said, laughing.

She dug her elbows into his ribs and slipped out of his grasp. 'I mean it, Jordan.'

'Prove it,' he said challengingly, advancing towards her with his eyes sparkling.

She threw some paper towels at him but he evaded them easily and she dodged behind one of the laundry baskets, laughing and gasping for breath.

'Jordan, you're mad!'

'Certifiable,' he replied, circling round the basket after her.

'This is crazy!' she protested, quickly retreating the other way.

'Completely and utterly,' he said, and then made a lunge. 'Got you!'

And he had.

'Jordan, don't!' she exclaimed, trying to twist away from him as his lips slowly traced the outline of her collar-bone and then began a downward slide into the deep V of her blouse. 'You promised you wouldn't touch me. You promised you wouldn't even kiss me on the cheek.'

'Now that definitely must have been some other bloke,' he murmured with a slight smile, before he gently brushed her lips with his own.

The effect was electrifying and when he deepened the kiss it was even more so.

You are insane, her mind whispered as all her resolve seemed to melt in an instant and her mouth opened willingly to accommodate his probing tongue. What are you doing? her heart asked as his hands slid up her sides to caress the tautness of her breasts through her silk blouse and she convulsed and arched herself against him.

Stop him, she told herself as she heard him give a sigh that was halfway to a groan when he pulled her hard against himself and she felt not only his arousal but her own moist response.

'Jordan—no,' she moaned against his throat, and heard him chuckle.

Dear God, what was she doing? she asked herself as her fingers moved of their own accord to lock themselves around his neck. If she didn't stop him soon they'd be making love on the changing-room floor.

'Enjoying yourself, Dr Fraser?'

She jumped and turned, only to flush scarlet. They weren't alone. Peter Thornton and the three hospital board members were standing in the doorway, and there was clear disapproval written all over their faces.

Swiftly she slipped out of Jordan's grasp. 'Peter—'

'We came to congratulate Dr Marshall on his remarkable skill,' he continued tightly, 'but it would appear that his head of department has her own very particular way of bestowing praise.'

Without another word, the four men banged out of the changing room and Claire groaned.

'Oh, God, I'm sorry,' Jordan began, his cheeks almost as red as hers. 'I didn't think—'

'First your damn motorbike and now this,' she said and sighed. Then she started to laugh. 'If I were the suspicious type I might start to wonder if you were actually deliberately trying to make me look ridiculous in order to get my job!'

His face whitened in an instant and anger appeared in his blue eyes. 'Don't you dare think that—not even for a second!'

'Jordan—'

'What kind of man do you think I am?' he demanded. 'Do you honestly believe that I'd set you up?'

'Jordan, I was joking,' she exclaimed, totally bemused by his outburst. '*Joking.*'

'Well, I'm not laughing,' he snapped. 'I do *not* want your job. No matter what anyone might ever say to you, I do *not* want your job—not now, not ever!'

'OK, OK,' she said soothingly. 'You don't have to yell at me—I get the message.'

His jaw clenched. 'Claire—'

The changing-room door swung open.

'Mrs Harding's arrived,' Debbie Carlton announced. 'Do you want Bill to pre-med her, Jordan?'

He struggled with himself for a moment. 'Yes...please.'

Debbie threw him a curious glance. 'You OK?'

'Fine,' he said with an effort. 'Just fine. I'll be with you in a minute.'

She nodded and withdrew and he ran a hand through his blond hair.

'Claire, I'm sorry. Sorry for yelling at you, sorry for giving Peter the opportunity—'

'It's OK—really, it is,' she interrupted, seeing the concern in his eyes. 'We shouldn't have been fooling about, but it's done. Forget it.'

'I wasn't fooling,' he said, his eyes fixed on her. 'I was deadly serious.'

A deep flush of colour crossed her cheeks and she clasped her hands tightly. 'Jordan—'

He swore as the changing-room door swung open yet again.

'Sorry to interrupt again,' Debbie said, 'but Mrs Harding's embryos have come down from the lab, and Bill would like to know how much longer you're going to be, Jordan.'

'He's just coming,' Claire replied, making her way to the door.

'Claire.'

She paused. His voice was soft, pleading, but she didn't turn around.

'Claire, we have to talk.'

They did, she knew they did, but she swung out of the changing room without a backward glance.

'I thought I'd be seeing Dr Marshall today,' Mary Bell said as she sat down.

'I'm afraid he's busy in Theatre right now so he asked me to see you instead,' Claire replied. 'I hope you don't mind.'

'Of course I don't.' Mary beamed.

Claire smiled inwardly. She doubted whether it would matter to Mary Bell if she was seen by an orang-utan at the moment. Ever since Jordan had told her she was pregnant she'd been over the moon.

'No problems, Mary?' she asked.

'A bit of morning sickness, but apart from that I feel wonderful.'

'Good.' Claire smiled as she got to her feet. 'Now, if you would just get up onto the couch, I'll give you a quick examination to check that everything's OK.'

It was, and Mary sighed with relief.

'When's my next appointment, Doctor?' she asked as she began to pull on her clothes.

Claire picked up Jordan's appointment book and leafed through it. 'The seventeenth of March, and if everything's fine you won't have to see us again.'

'But I thought— Won't you or Dr Marshall be seeing me through my pregnancy?' Mary said in surprise.

Claire shook her head. 'Once you get to between twelve and sixteen weeks our maternity department takes over.'

'But, that means you won't see the result of all your hard work,' Mary said.

'We hear about it,' Claire replied, 'and some proud parents bring their children in to see us, but our part is solely to try to ensure that you get pregnant. Maternity does all the rest.'

'Well, I think that's a shame,' Mary declared. 'And I'll most certainly bring my baby in to see you.'

'I'll look forward to it,' Claire said cheerfully.

'Will I see Dr Marshall when I come in next time?' Mary asked, and then flushed. 'It's not that I mind seeing you, Dr Fraser,' she added quickly, 'but he's such a lovely man, isn't he? The kind of man you feel you can trust.'

He was, Claire thought as she walked with Mary to the lift, but was trust enough? He'd told her time and time again since they'd started dating that they could make a relationship work, and she wanted to believe him. She so wanted to believe him, but...

With a deep sigh she turned, intending to go back to her room, only to come to a halt as she saw Peter Thornton walking down the corridor towards her.

'Come to tear me off a strip, have you?' she said dryly.

'Not at all,' he replied, with a smile that failed to reach his eyes. 'I just thought I'd pay you a social call.'

Peter didn't make social calls. Peter wouldn't recognise a social call if it sat up and bit him, but if that was the way he wanted to play it then who was she to argue?

'Would you like a coffee?' she asked. 'I was just about to get one.'

He nodded, but when they reached Roz's office a frown appeared on his face.

'Where's your secretary?'

'Probably in the store cupboard, making mad, passionate love to one of the porters,' Claire replied as she took two cups out of the cupboard.

'That's not funny,' he snapped. 'This office should never be left unattended during working hours.'

'I quite agree,' she said, putting a cup under the filter machine, 'but somebody's got to collect our reports from the lab, and as you won't allow me another secretary...'

Peter opened his mouth and then closed it again.

'Biscuit?' she said sweetly, holding out the tin to him. He took one silently.

'What do you really want, Peter?' she asked, as she gave him his coffee.

He took a sip, grimaced slightly and put it down. 'How's your new assistant settling in?'

'Fine.'

'No problems?'

Her eyebrows rose. 'Should there be?'

'I just wondered whether there might not be some friction between the two of you as he's more qualified than you are.'

She put down her own coffee carefully. 'Believe it or not, neither I nor Jordan is that petty. As for his qualifications—while I'll concede that his surgical skills are superior to mine in certain areas—'

'Ah.'

'And what's that supposed to mean?' she demanded.

'It's those skills that worry me,' he observed pensively. 'Think about it, Claire,' he continued as she opened her mouth to protest. 'To be your assistant can't be the most fulfilling experience in the world for a man of his calibre, and I would hate him to just take off one day when a permanent senior post becomes available, leaving you in the lurch.'

He was right—there was that possibility—but it was something she didn't care to think about right now.

'I'll worry about it when it happens,' she replied.

Peter gazed at her thoughtfully for a moment. 'Would it surprise you to know that I think I might have made a mistake in asking him to come here?'

It did surprise her but not for one second was she going to admit it.

'Surely you don't make mistakes, Peter?' she said with a malicious smile.

'Not often,' he replied, 'but when I do...' he smiled '...I always rectify them.'

Unaccountably she felt uneasy and when he walked to the door she followed him.

'Peter—'

'Just remember what I said, Claire,' he interrupted. 'Men like Jordan—they're ambitious, and their ambitions can make them unpredictable.'

A deep frown appeared on her forehead as Peter walked away. If she hadn't known better she would have sworn that he was truly concerned about her, but the only person Peter ever cared about was himself. If he was warning her about Jordan, it had to be because he had some ulterior motive.

But he's right about Jordan, isn't he? a tiny voice whispered. A temporary post, working for you, can't be very satisfying, and even if he stays for the rest of his contract he's going to leave. He's going to leave and you're never going to see him again.

Her heart contracted at the thought and suddenly she knew that she had to get away. For just a few minutes she had to get away from a department that suddenly felt overwhelmingly claustrophobic.

Quickly she made for the stairs and she didn't stop until she rounded the corner on the first floor and cannoned straight into Anne Sommerville.

'Hey, what's the rush?' Anne exclaimed.

'Sorry,' Claire mumbled, and tried to push past her, only to feel Anne's hand on her arm.

'What's up, Claire?'

'Nothing,' she protested. 'I want... I just need a little fresh air, that's all.'

The head of ICBU gazed at her intently for a moment and then shook her head.

'I'm fine,' Claire insisted. 'I'm OK, I'm...'

She came to a halt, appallingly aware that she was close to tears, and without a word Anne steered her into her office and shut the door.

'OK, take the weight off your feet, take a deep breath and tell me what's wrong.'

For a second Claire didn't move and then she sat down limply. 'I'm just a bit tired, that's all. It's been one hell of a week.'

'It's only Monday, love,' Anne replied. 'You're going to have to come up with something a whole lot better than that to fool me. It's Jordan, isn't it?' she continued. 'You're falling in love with Jordan.'

'That's the most ridiculous thing I've ever heard,' Claire retorted.

Anne chuckled and then her face grew serious. 'Look, Claire, I know I have the reputation of being a dreadful gossip—and I am—but you're my friend. Whatever you tell me will go no further—I promise.'

Claire gazed at her uncertainly for a moment and sighed. 'I can't deny that I like him, Anne. In fact, I like him a lot.'

'And?'

'He says he wants me. He says that we could make a relationship work, but…'

'You're scared?' Anne asked gently.

Claire nodded. 'I don't want to be hurt again. I don't want to turn round one day and find him looking at me the way Max sometimes did, as though I were a total stranger.'

'But—'

'Anne, I was married to Max for five years but our marriage was over long before he finally left me. At the beginning…' She sighed and shook her head. 'At the beginning he loved me enough to argue, to beg me to spend more time with him, but after a while he stopped arguing. I thought it was because he'd accepted that my work was important to me. It was only later that I realised it was because he just didn't care any more.'

Anne frowned. 'Do you love him, Claire?'

She gazed down, her face troubled. 'I don't know. I haven't even allowed myself to consider it, you see. I know I want him—'

'Then go for it,' Anne interrupted firmly.

'What if it didn't work?' Claire murmured. 'What if we make one another desperately unhappy?'

'You're never going to know unless you try.'

'Then how come you haven't tried?' Claire protested. 'How come you're divorced, and happy to be on your own?'

'Am I?'

'Of course you are,' Claire said. 'You're always telling me how great it is to be able to do what you want, go where you want.'

'Claire, I'm forty-seven years old and do you know what

I've got to show for my life? One divorce, no children and a canary.'

'But you're head of ICBU—'

'Which I leave every night to go home to an empty flat. Take a bit of advice from a friend, Claire. Don't close your mind to a future because of the past.'

Claire stared at her in surprise.

She had always thought that Anne had it all—a successful career, a wide circle of friends and a great social life—and yet she'd just implied that she'd swap the lot for a man in her life.

'But, Anne—'

'Sorry to interrupt you, Dr Sommerville,' a staff nurse said breathlessly as she threw open the door, 'but Baby Johnson's BP's down and his cardiac output's way up.'

Anne got to her feet.

'Think about what I said, Claire,' she said as she went to the door. 'Opportunities like this don't come round too often and if you think there's a chance that it might work—even the slimmest chance—then take it or you'll always regret it.'

Claire frowned as she made her way back up the stairs. It was easy for Anne to say take a chance. She wouldn't be the one taking it. She wouldn't be the one who would have to find out the hard way whether taking that chance would lead to happiness or heartbreak.

Unconsciously she shook her head. The risks were too great, the price she might have to pay was too high.

'I've been looking for you.'

She turned to see Jordan, standing behind her.

'Claire, we have to talk,' he said gently.

They did, and she knew he wasn't going to like what she had to say. She cleared her throat. 'Would you like to come to dinner tonight?'

'Dinner?' he repeated.

'You said we must talk so would around half seven be OK?'

'Half past seven would be fine,' he replied.

There was no going back now, she thought as she watched him walk away. Tonight she would tell him that she was sorry. She would tell him that one of them had to be sensible. She would tell him that she wanted no more flowers or visits to the cinema. It was over, finished.

It was the right thing to do, she told herself. It was the sensible thing to do, and if she felt more miserable than she'd ever done in her life then she'd get over it. She'd got over Max so she could get over Jordan.

But she didn't feel at all sensible by the time the hands on her sitting room clock had crept to half past seven.

Three times she had lifted the phone to tell Jordan that she'd changed her mind and dinner was off, and three times she'd put it back down again.

You're behaving like a teenager on your first date, she told herself as she heard her doorbell ring and reluctantly went to answer it. But she wasn't, and she knew she wasn't. A teenager didn't know how the date was going to end but she did, and the prospect was an overwhelmingly depressing one.

'Am I too early?' Jordan asked as she opened the door and stared at him, her cheeks flushed, her grey eyes strained.

'No, of course not—come in,' she replied, stepping back awkwardly.

'Something smells nice,' he commented as he followed her down the hall.

'It's the beef curry. Oh, hell,' she added in panic, 'I never thought to ask—maybe you don't like curry—'

'I do—I like it very much.'

She managed to smile. 'Would you like a drink? I've whisky, vodka, beer—'

'Nothing for me, thanks.'

Quickly she walked across to her stereo and began flicking through her CDs.

'The curry will be ready in about fifteen minutes so would you like to listen to some music while we wait? Or we could watch some TV, if you'd prefer. There's a wild-life documentary on tonight that's supposed to be really good—'

'Claire.'

His hands had encircled her waist and she could feel his breath warm on the back of her neck.

'Claire, I didn't come here tonight to listen to your stereo or to watch a wildlife documentary on TV,' he said softly. 'You know why I came.'

Her heart was hammering so hard against her ribcage that she thought for one awful moment she might faint. Desperately she took a deep breath, swallowed hard and turned.

'Jordan, I'm sorry,' she began hesitantly. 'I've thought and thought...but it isn't going to work. No matter how we might both feel, it just isn't going to work. We'll hurt one another, I know we will, and I don't want that—I couldn't bear it.'

He gazed back at her, his face totally unreadable, and then he nodded.

'OK, my lovely,' he said, releasing her. 'How long did you say it would be before dinner was ready?'

She stared at him in confusion. 'Fifteen minutes, but—'

'Any idea which channel the wildlife documentary is on?' he asked, picking up the TV guide.

'Jordan, I've just said that I don't want our relationship to develop into anything...physical,' she said awkwardly. 'Don't...don't you care?'

'Of course I care,' he replied, 'but it's your decision. Oh great,' he added, as he switched on the TV. 'We've only missed five minutes.'

'But, Jordan—'

He glanced over his shoulder at her, his eyebrows raised. 'Yes?'

She tried to meet his eyes, and couldn't.

'I thought…' She bit her lip. 'I thought you might argue, try to talk me round.'

'I wouldn't dream of pressurising you,' he said firmly.

'I didn't mean that I wanted you to pressurise me,' she protested. 'I meant…I just meant…'

'Hmm?' he murmured, his eyes fixed on the TV.

'Oh, forget it,' she retorted angrily. 'Just forget it, and watch your damn wildlife documentary!'

She turned on her heel and stormed into the kitchen. She'd thought he'd care, but he obviously didn't. She'd thought he'd try to persuade her to change her mind. Thought—or hoped? her mind whispered, and she didn't like the answer her heart gave one bit.

Angrily she pulled two plates out of the cupboard, only to jump as she felt a kiss on the back of her neck.

'Was that what you had in mind when you said you expected me to argue?' he asked as she whirled furiously. 'Or maybe…maybe it was something more like this.'

Without a word of warning, he pulled her into his arms and kissed her until her knees felt like water and she thought her heart would explode.

'Well?' he asked, laughter plain in his voice.

She gazed up at him in a daze.

'You rat!' she said slowly, and began to laugh. 'You unprincipled, devious rat! That wasn't what I meant—you know it wasn't.' She came to a halt as he stretched past her and switched off the stove. 'Jordan…Jordan, what are you doing?'

'What it looks like,' he declared, shrugging himself out of his jacket and unknotting his tie. 'You clearly need a lot of persuading, and you know what they say—actions speak louder than words.'

She backed out into the hall, shaking her head. 'No, Jordan.'

'Don't you mean yes?' he said, pulling his shirt over his head sending the buttons ricocheting in every direction.

'Jordan, be sensible,' she protested, starting to laugh again. 'It won't work—you and I.'

'Who says?' he asked, his eyes warm as he advanced on her determinedly.

'I say—and you said so, too, until you went completely insane,' she said, retreating from him, only to find herself trapped in the doorway to her bedroom. He reached out and caught her hand, his face suddenly serious.

'I was wrong—so wrong. I love you, Claire Fraser. Can't we try—can't we at least give it a try?'

She gazed up at him. God, but she wanted him—she wanted him so much. Maybe if she tried harder this time she could make it work. Maybe if she didn't give all of her heart this time but kept a little part of it back until she was sure, really sure, it would be all right.

'It's your decision, Claire,' he said, as though he'd read her mind.

And it *was* her decision. She knew he would go if she asked him to, but she didn't want him to go.

'Well, Claire?' he said softly, and she smiled.

'You'd have made one hell of an insurance salesman, Jordan.'

He laughed, took her into his arms and made love to her.

Every touch of his hands and mouth was unbelievably gentle, as though he sensed her lingering uncertainty, but she didn't want him to be gentle. She wanted him to take her swiftly, roughly, to blot out all her doubts and fears.

'Jordan, please,' she gasped raggedly, as he teased her nipples into aching hardness with his mouth.

'Patience,' he whispered hoarsely, as he caressed her inner thighs with his lips and tongue until she groaned with desperate need.

'Now, Jordan, now,' she begged, and her breathing came in great shuddering gasps as she squirmed beneath him, urging, entreating.

But when he finally moved within her, deep and powerful and urgent, although her cry of elation matched his own, suddenly, and without knowing why, tears began to trickle slowly down her cheeks.

Gradually, slowly, her breathing returned to normal, and when she opened her eyes it was to find Jordan, gazing down at her with concern.

'Are you OK?' he asked gently.

She hadn't meant this to happen. She had told herself that this must never happen, but it had, and she managed to smile. 'I'm fine, couldn't be better, but—'

'Hey, it wasn't that bad, was it?' he said, uncertainty plain in his voice.

She shook her head. 'Jordan…what we just did… Was it the start of something or just a one-night-stand?'

'We weren't actually standing, if you recall,' he said, grinning. 'Maybe you'd like to try it that way now?'

'Jordan, I'm serious,' she declared. 'Are we talking a one-off thing here or what?'

He traced the outline of her jaw with his finger and smiled. 'I was kind of hoping for the "or what".'

'Meaning?'

'That you'd move in with me or I'd move in with you.'

'For how long?'

'I wasn't planning on for just a couple of days, if that's what you're thinking,' he said, ruffled.

She took a deep breath. 'OK, you can move in with me.'

'W-what?' he stammered.

'I said you can move in with me.'

He knew he should have felt elated—overjoyed—but somehow he didn't, although he managed to smile as her eyebrows rose.

'You don't look too happy,' she said.

'I'm just a bit stunned, that's all,' he said with perfect truth.

'But isn't this what you want?' she protested.

It was, but as he took her in his arms and kissed her he couldn't help feeling that something was missing. Even when he made love to her again he still had the strangest feeling that something was missing.

CHAPTER EIGHT

CLAIRE'S eyes swept round her sitting room and her jaw set.

Six weeks. Jordan had only been living with her for six weeks and yet already her flat was a shambles. Gone was the pristine neatness she had so cherished, and in its place chaos reigned in the form of Jordan's discarded clothes and abandoned books.

'Claire, have you seen my other brown shoe?'

She gritted her teeth. 'Try the bathroom.'

'The bathroom?'

She gritted her teeth even harder. 'I saw a brown shoe in the bathroom—'

'Fine!'

Oh, no, it wasn't, she decided. It wasn't fine at all.

'OK, that's me.' Jordan beamed as he hopped into the sitting room, pulling on his shoe. 'Ready to go?'

'To go?' she echoed. 'You mean, you're actually going to walk out that door, leaving my flat looking like this?'

He glanced around, puzzled. 'Looking like what?'

She clenched her fists tight against her sides and struggled to remain calm. 'Jordan, my flat looks like a bomb has hit it.'

'Well, I've got to admit that you're not the tidiest woman in the world to live with—'

'It's not funny, Jordan,' she broke in as he grinned at her. 'You're a slob—you know that, don't you? You never pick up a book, you leave your clothes lying all over the place, you've made four rings on my coffee-table, ruined two of my saucepans—'

'Claire—'

133

'And if you think I'm going to continue to tidy up after you, you need your head examined,' she stormed. 'I am not your mother and I am not, thank God, your wife!'

The words were out of her mouth before she had time to think and she regretted them immediately, but it was too late to take them back. He was already heading for the door and anger flared within her.

'Don't you dare walk away from me when I'm talking to you!' she yelled after him.

He turned, his face cold, shuttered. 'I'm going to be late for work.'

'Is that all you have to say?' she gasped. 'Jordan, we've got to discuss this—'

'What's there to discuss?' he asked. 'You've already made your point.'

Something about his face told her that she'd made more of a point than she'd ever intended, and she grasped his arm.

'Jordan, I didn't mean—'

'I've got a consultation in twenty minutes, and you're due in Theatre to do the laparoscopic egg collection on Helen Elliot,' he interrupted, infuriatingly calm.

She let go of his arm, and her voice when she spoke was tight.

'Fine. Great. But let's get one thing straight. We can't go on living like this, Jordan.'

'I agree,' he said evenly. 'We can't.'

Her heart skipped a beat. He was gazing down at her with an unnervingly familiar expression. It was an expression she had seen all too often on Max's face when she'd tried to discuss something with him and he hadn't wanted to listen.

'Jordan—'

He didn't even wait to hear what she'd been going to say. He just turned on his heel and went out the door. For a moment she didn't move and then she hurried after him.

'What time will you be back tonight?' she asked, forcing herself into a calmness she was very far from feeling.

'I don't know.'

His voice was casual, dismissive, and her jaw tightened. Dammit, why should she feel guilty about complaining? It was her home he was messing up, her home he was disrupting. What she'd said was the truth, and it had needed saying.

'It would be helpful if you could be just a little more specific,' she said, her voice sharp. 'It's my turn to cook tonight.'

'Don't bother cooking for me,' he replied as he got onto his bike and switched on the ignition. 'If I want anything I'll fix it for myself.'

She stared at him impotently and then her temper reached breaking-point.

'Oh, for God's sake, Jordan, don't sulk. I hate it when men sulk!'

He glanced over his shoulder at her, his blue eyes cold. 'And I hate it when women nag.'

Her jaw dropped. She opened her mouth and closed it again, and by the time she'd thought of a stinging reply he had disappeared in a cloud of exhaust fumes.

Nag, she thought furiously as she got into her car and slammed the door shut. He didn't know the meaning of the word, but he sure as heck was going to find out if he didn't shape up his ideas—and fast.

The traffic on Byres Road was hell, and it was even worse on Great Western Road so that it was gone ten past nine when she finally flew breathlessly into the changing room.

'I know, I know,' she exclaimed, as Debbie stared in surprise at her. 'Mr Jarvis has a heart bypass scheduled for nine-thirty and he'll have my guts for garters if I run into his time. Tell Bill I'm here and ask him to pre-med Helen Elliot for me.'

Debbie looked uncomfortable. 'He's already done it.'

'But—'

'Jordan's nine o'clock appointment cancelled, and when you were late he said he'd perform Mrs Elliot's laparoscopic egg collection.'

'Oh, did he?' Claire replied with a glittering smile. 'Well, you can tell Dr Marshall that his presence is not required— I'm doing the op.'

'Claire—'

'Tell him, Debbie.'

The theatre sister disappeared in a flurry of green, and Claire whipped into one of the cubicles and began to drag off her clothes.

The nerve of the man, the sheer nerve of him. She was head of the department, not him, and he had no right to make decisions like that. OK, so Helen Elliot was one of his patients, but he'd said four days ago that he couldn't do the retrieval and it wasn't her fault that she was late. Maybe if he cleaned up after himself, instead of just throwing everything onto the floor—

'Claire.'

Her mouth tightened as she emerged from the cubicle. 'Yes?'

'Claire, it's a quarter past nine, and I'm already scrubbed up—'

'So?' she interrupted, her tone dangerous.

'Wouldn't it be more sensible if I did the op?'

Of course it would be more sensible, but right now she didn't feel sensible.

'I'll be ready in five minutes.'

'But, Claire—'

'If you've got nothing better to do—and you plainly haven't—you can assist if you want.'

His lips thinned to a fine line. 'Fine.'

Quickly she turned on the tap and began to scrub up, all too conscious that his blue eyes were fixed on her. Well, he could stand there until the cows came home as far as she was concerned. She was head of this department, not him, and it was about time he realised that.

'Mrs Elliot is ready, Claire,' Debbie declared, pushing open the changing-room door with her elbow. Claire nodded, fastened her mask and swept past Jordan without a word.

'Hi, there, Claire.' Bill Morton smiled as he adjusted the blood pressure monitor. 'We'd just about given you up.'

'So I heard,' she said tightly. 'How's Helen?'

'Sleeping like a baby,' the anaesthetist replied.

Quickly Claire made her first incision into Helen's abdomen and then inserted the small specialised telescope. A tiny cut in Helen's abdominal wall enabled her to insert a smaller probe so that she could move the ovaries during the egg recovery. Then, with a needle carefully inserted through the abdominal wall into the pelvis, she was ready.

'Managing OK?' Jordan asked.

She drew in her breath sharply. Was he presuming to give her lessons in surgery now?

Without lifting her head, she swiftly collected the fluid from the ovary into the syringe and examined it to see how many eggs she had collected. Six. That was a good sign.

'Are you going to flush the follicle to see if there are any more?' Jordan continued.

Her head came up at that.

'No, I'm not.' She glared. 'I'm just going to leave them there so that one of them can develop into an ectopic pregnancy. Of course I'm going to flush the damn follicle!'

'I was only asking—'

'Then don't!' she snapped. 'If you've got nothing better to do other than make facetious comments you can suture for me.'

His eyes narrowed and when he spoke his voice was a good deal harder than hers. 'I'll suture for you with pleasure if it will put an end to your infernal sniping.'

A sharp retort sprang to her lips but she crushed it

quickly, all too aware that Bill and Debbie were gazing at them in wide-eyed fascination.

How could this morning's argument about the state of her flat have turned so quickly into a full-scale row? she wondered as she picked up the syringe after she'd completed the procedure and swung out of the operating theatre.

Because you're exhausted, she answered herself as she made her way to the lab, physically and mentally exhausted. Your job's getting on top of you, and as for Jordan…

She sighed. She'd been trying so hard to make their relationship work—trying too hard.

That was why she hadn't spoken to him before about his untidiness. She hadn't wanted to say anything, or do anything, that might drive him away. For the last six weeks she'd been walking on eggshells around him, and her nerves were in shreds.

'You're looking a bit frayed, Claire,' Sybil observed as soon as she saw her.

Claire fixed the senior lab technician with her widest smile.

'It's the time of the month, Sybil,' she lied. 'I don't think any of us are at our best then.'

Sybil didn't look one bit convinced and quickly Claire got onto one of the stools and prepared to begin the delicate task of taking just one sperm at a time from Alan Elliot's sample and injecting it directly under the outer protective covering of each of his wife's eggs.

'I thought the Elliots were Jordan's patients?' Sybil said, glancing over Claire's shoulder at the name-tag on the syringe.

'They are.'

'Then shouldn't he be doing—?'

'He's busy, Sybil,' Claire interrupted, 'and so am I.'

Hot colour flooded into the lab technician's plump cheeks and she flounced away with a toss of her head.

That wasn't very clever, Claire, she told herself as she

returned to her work. Sybil was the worst gossip in the hospital and she would bet money that within the hour the whole of the Ravelston would know that she was in a bad mood and would be busy speculating why.

She shook her head. Concentrate, Claire, concentrate. ICSI had been the most important advance in the treatment of male infertility in the last two decades, but it didn't stand a hope in hell of succeeding if the doctor who was doing it had her mind on other things.

At long last she eased her aching neck muscles and sat back. It was done. It was now just a question of waiting to see whether the eggs were fertilised or not.

'Finished?'

She turned in her seat and found herself gazing into a pair of blue eyes.

She nodded and then moistened her lips. She wasn't going to apologise for what she'd said earlier in the flat, but even she knew that she'd been behaving like a bitch ever since.

'Jordan, I'm sorry about what I said to you in the theatre.'

'Right now we've got bigger problems,' he replied. 'The Hardings are due in my office in fifteen minutes and I've got Liz's results back from the lab. The embryos didn't take.'

She pushed her hair back from her shoulders and sighed. 'We did warn her that she only had a one in eight chance of it working and this is just her first treatment—'

'Will you sit in with me when I tell her?' he broke in. 'I've got a feeling she might need some feminine support.'

'Of course I will,' she replied, 'but it's going to be rough, Jordan.'

It was.

Liz stared at the two of them blankly and then shook her head.

'You're wrong—you're definitely wrong. I'm pregnant—I *feel* pregnant.'

'I'm sorry, Liz,' Claire said gently, 'but the test was conclusive. None of the embryos have taken.'

'But they must have taken. My period hasn't started—'

'It's just late,' Claire interrupted, her eyes full of compassion. 'Sometimes your body plays cruel tricks on you, and I'm afraid this is just one of those times.'

Liz shook her head again and tears welled in her eyes. 'You've made a mistake—you must have made a mistake!'

Her husband was clearly as deeply distressed as she was, and when Jordan gazed helplessly across at Claire she got to her feet and went quickly round the desk.

'I wish it was a mistake, Liz,' she said softly. 'You've no idea how much I wish it was a mistake, but it's not— you're not pregnant.'

Liz began to sob as though her heart would break and Claire put her arms around her and hugged her tight.

No matter how many times this happened—and it happened far too often for her own peace of mind—it didn't make it any easier to deal with.

Bob Harding tugged at his collar and swallowed with difficulty. 'Why didn't it work?'

'The trouble is that IVF is still very much an experimental treatment,' Jordan replied. 'Sometimes none of the eggs become fertilised. Sometimes the embryos fail to develop normally and aren't suitable for transfer. And sometimes, as in Liz's case, the embryos are transferred but they just don't stick.'

'Does that mean that if we keep on trying one of the embryos might eventually stay where it should?' Bob asked, hope appearing in his eyes, and Jordan sighed.

'I've got to be honest with you, Bob. While it's true that the more times you try the better your chances are, we've discovered that if you haven't conceived after four attempts the likelihood of success isn't good.'

Liz lifted a tear-stained face to Claire. 'I want to try again.'

'Oh, Liz, I understand how you feel,' Claire said, pressing a handkerchief into her hand, 'but it's far too early to be thinking about another course.'

'We've got the money,' Bob began. 'We can pay—'

'It isn't a question of money,' Jordan interrupted firmly. 'Going through an IVF course is a harrowing experience and when it doesn't work you need time to come to terms with it. If you want to try again we'll help you, but right now I want you both to take time to grieve.'

'But—'

'Dr Marshall's right, Liz,' Claire said softly. 'The best thing the two of you can do is to go home and give yourselves time and space to get over this.'

There was a long silence in the consulting room after the Hardings had left and then Jordan gave a short laugh.

'Now's your opportunity to say "I told you so."'

Claire rubbed her tired eyes. 'I wouldn't dream of it. Not only would it be a really rotten thing to say but it's also far too early in the treatment to write it off as a failure.'

He gazed at her for a moment and then shook his head. 'You really mean that, don't you?'

A small smile curved her lips. 'The trouble with you, Jordan Marshall, is that you don't know me very well.'

His blue eyes caught and held hers. 'The trouble with you, Claire Fraser, is that sometimes I feel like I don't know you at all.'

Her heart turned over. Max had said exactly the same thing just before he'd left. And suddenly she found herself remembering other things—the half-started conversations that Jordan had never finished, the times when she'd caught him gazing at her with a thoughtful, puzzled expression, only for him to look away quickly as soon as her eyes had met his.

'Jordan—' She came to a halt as the phone rang and he reached for it.

'It's for you,' he said after a few seconds. 'A and E,' he added as her eyebrows rose enquiringly.

She took the phone and listened with a sinking heart as the registrar gave her the details.

'What's up?' Jordan asked when she put down the phone with a groan.

'It's Gillian White—one of my POS patients. She's just been brought into A and E with a suspected ectopic.'

'Symptoms?'

'Sickness, diarrhoea, a lot of pain on one side of her abdomen. She's also bleeding a little from her vagina.'

'How far on is she?'

'Seven weeks.'

'Sounds like a definite ectopic, then, and not a miscarriage,' he observed, and saw her frown. 'Want me to come down to A and E with you?'

She glanced up at him in surprise. 'Are you sure? I mean, I thought after my performance this morning...'

'What performance?' He smiled. 'That was just you, being your normal self.'

She stuck out her tongue at him. 'Funny guy. OK, let's go.'

The registrar was waiting for them at the entrance to A and E, his face worried.

'We've done a blood test, and she's definitely pregnant,' he declared, 'so I'm afraid it must be an ectopic and not a miscarriage.'

'Damn, damn, *damn*!' Claire exclaimed in frustration. 'And she was doing so well.'

'Has she had anything to eat this morning?' Jordan asked.

'Tea and toast,' the registrar replied, 'but I'd say she brought most of that up about ten minutes ago so you should be able to operate OK. I've alerted Theatre to expect you.'

'I'd better have a word with her.' Claire sighed.

Gillian was lying on one of the trolleys, her face white and drawn, but as soon as she saw Claire her eyes lit up.

'Doctor, they're saying something's wrong—'

'I'm afraid there is,' Claire broke in quickly. 'It seems that your fertilised egg hasn't implanted itself into your uterus but has gone into one of your Fallopian tubes instead. We're going to have to remove it, Gillian.'

The girl shook her head wildly. 'You're not going to take my baby away!'

'Gillian, we have to,' Claire said, her voice gentle but firm. 'If we leave it there you could die and the foetus can't possibly grow normally.'

'It might...'

'It won't,' Claire insisted. 'I'm sorry, but we have to remove it.'

Tears rolled slowly down Gillian's face. 'Can't you wait until my husband gets here? He's at work but one of the nurses said she'd ring him.'

Claire glanced across at Jordan and he shook his head.

'Her blood pressure's going through the roof,' he murmured under his breath.

Claire gripped Gillian's hand tightly. 'I'm sorry, but we can't wait. We have to operate now.'

'But—'

'Gillian, I know it seems like the end of the world right now,' Claire said softly, 'but we have to think of your health.'

'I don't care about my health,' she sobbed. 'I want to have a baby—this baby!'

'Gillian—'

'Why did this have to happen to me?' the girl protested. 'Other women can have babies. Other women—awful, horrible women—can breed like rabbits and I can't even have one! Isn't there anything you can do? Can't you take it out of the tube and put it back in the right place?'

Claire shook her head. 'I'm afraid the foetus wouldn't survive. It wouldn't have any blood supply, you see.'

Gillian turned on her side and sobbed as though her heart would break, and Claire quickly went out of the cubicle. For a moment she leant against the wall with her eyes shut, and when she opened them she saw Jordan, gazing at her with concern.

'Are you all right?'

'Oh, Jordan, this is turning out to be such a bloody awful day!'

'Would you like me to do the op for you?' he said.

For a moment she was tempted and then she shook her head. 'I'll do it, but would you assist?'

'No problem,' he replied, and wearily Claire led the way to the operating theatre.

'Back again?' Debbie said with a smile as soon as she saw them. 'You must be developing a love of the place.'

'Not so you'd notice,' Claire sighed.

Debbie chuckled and then her face grew serious.

'I'd better warn you that Mr Finlay's kicking up merry hell at having to wait to perform his hip replacement.'

'Mr Finlay can stick his stethoscope where the sun don't shine,' Claire declared sourly. 'Would you ask Bill to pre-med Gillian as soon as she arrives from A and E? And you'd better make sure we've got plenty of type A blood on standby. Ectopics can bleed like crazy.'

'I'll see to it,' the theatre sister replied, departing in a rustle of starched cotton.

Silently Claire and Jordan changed into their theatre clothes and scrubbed up.

'All set?' Jordan asked when Claire finally pulled on her surgical gloves.

'As I'll ever be,' she murmured.

'You just can't keep away from me, can you, Claire?' Bill Morton beamed as soon as he saw her. 'Must be my fatal charm.'

'It's not your charm, Bill,' she replied. 'It's something about the way you twirl those dials—it drives a girl crazy.'

They all laughed and Claire knew that it wasn't because they were hard and unfeeling but that if they didn't find humour even in the grimmest of situations they would never be able to survive.

'BP now improved, heart rate fine, lungs OK,' Bill said at last. 'I'm ready when you are.'

Swiftly Claire made her first incision and eased her way through into the uterus.

'How does it look?' Jordan asked.

'It's definitely an ectopic,' she replied. 'I can see the little blighter lodged in the Fallopian tube. The tube itself is slightly damaged but...'

She came to a halt and frowned.

'She can still get pregnant with only one tube,' Jordan observed.

'I know,' she said, 'but if I take out the embryo, without removing the tube, it will give her a much better chance of having a normal pregnancy later.'

'It's a tricky op, Claire, and it could also put her at risk of having another ectopic,' he pointed out.

'I can do it,' she answered, 'and the risk would only be one in twenty-five. Pretty good odds, considering.'

'Then go for it.'

She lifted her eyebrows. 'We're agreed?'

'Do you think I'm stupid enough to argue with a woman holding a scalpel?' He grinned.

She shook her head and laughed. 'Have we plenty of blood, Debbie?'

'Masses,' she answered.

Claire took a deep breath and began. It was tricky work, made even more nerve-racking by Jordan's watchful gaze, but eventually she became so absorbed in her task that she forgot all about him.

This was what she had trained for during all those years at medical school and, although she could sympathise with Gillian's devastation, the challenge of removing the embryo, whilst leaving the Fallopian tube intact, was one she could not help but relish.

'Well done,' Jordan murmured, when the embryo finally came away and a smile of satisfaction appeared on her face.

'Not bad, if I say so myself,' she declared.

*   *   *

It was the single bright moment in what turned out to be an exhausting and particularly stressful morning.

The lab phoned to tell her that none of their samples could be tested until the end of the week because Men's Surgical had sent down an emergency batch that had to be tested immediately. Roz had somehow managed to give two sets of patients exactly the same appointment, and by the time Claire had pacified them there was nothing left in the canteen but curled-up sandwiches.

The afternoon didn't get any better. George Finlay tore a strip off her for invading his operating time, and when she told him that in her opinion an ectopic pregnancy took precedence over a hip replacement he slammed the phone down on her. Even Jordan provided no respite to her depression. Whenever she saw him he seemed preoccupied and distant, and answered her comments in monosyllables.

'Thank God today's over,' Roz said in a heartfelt voice when Claire eventually appeared in her office to say that her last patient had gone. 'Do you realise it's half past seven?'

Claire groaned. 'Is it only that? I was sure it must be midnight at least.'

'I'm really sorry about the Wilkinsons and the Clarks—'

'Forget it,' Claire said. 'This hasn't been one of my better days either.'

'Well, I'm going home to soak in a long hot bath,' her secretary declared as they walked together out to the car park.

'Sounds wonderful,' Claire said enviously.

'You can do the same,' Roz pointed out, and Claire smiled but said nothing.

After a day like today she wouldn't be at all surprised if she got home to discover that Jordan had used up all the hot water.

Jordan. A deep sigh escaped her as she drove through the dark Glasgow streets. He was probably sitting in the flat, expecting her to resume this morning's argument, and right now she felt so wrung out that she could barely think, far less argue.

Please just let him apologise and promise to be tidier from now on, she thought as she drew her car to a halt outside the flat. Please let him just listen to me calmly and rationally because I just can't face another row, not tonight.

But all thoughts of having a row disappeared when she let herself wearily into the flat. There wasn't a book or a piece of clothing to be seen, and when she went into the kitchen it was spotless.

'You've cleaned up,' she said in amazement as Jordan came out of the bathroom.

'Amazing what a bit of elbow grease and a vacuum can do, isn't it?' he said with a rueful smile.

'I'm pleased to see that you've finally realised that,' she said, kicking off her shoes.

'I'm sorry about the mess I've been leaving,' he continued. 'I told you I was impossible to live with, but I hadn't realised just how much.'

'Forget it,' she said, sitting down limply.

He looked at her for a moment and then sat down too. 'I'm afraid I don't think we can.'

'Of course we can,' she smiled. 'I don't like behaving like a bitch, but I won't be taken for granted either.'

'I accept that,' he said, 'but the trouble is that I don't think your outburst this morning was solely about how untidy I am.'

'Of course it was,' she protested, a deep feeling of unease creeping over her. 'I've worked hard to get my flat looking like this—'

'Listen to yourself, Claire,' he interrupted, his voice suddenly harsh. '*My* flat. And this morning it was *my* coffee-table, *my* saucepans.'

She gazed at him in bewilderment. 'But they are my things.'

'Then let's move upstairs to my place—or, better still, let's buy a new flat together and start from scratch.'

'But I don't want to move somewhere else,' she exclaimed. 'This is my home.'

He leant back in his seat, his face impassive. 'And what am I—the temporary stud?'

A deep flush of colour stained her cheeks. 'Of course you're not. That's a horrible thing to say.'

'It's more horrible to feel like it, believe me,' he said bitterly.

'Jordan—'

'Claire, will you marry me?'

She stared back at him in surprise. 'W-what?'

'I said, will you marry me?'

She got to her feet, completely thrown. 'What do we need to get married for? We're happy as we are—'

'Maybe you are,' he interrupted, 'but I want us to get married.'

'But *why*?' she protested.

His lips curled into a rueful smile. 'Isn't that what people usually do when they're in love?'

She shook her head vehemently. 'Jordan, I've been married before and it was a terrible mistake. I don't want to do it again.'

'Claire—'

'Marriage—it's not for me. I don't think I can handle that kind of commitment.'

'Isn't that supposed to be my line?' he observed, his mouth slightly twisted.

'W-what?' she stammered.

'The "I can't handle commitment" bit. Isn't that supposed to be the man's line?'

She bit her lip. 'Please don't mock me, Jordan.'

'I didn't mean to,' he said, his voice gentle, 'but the bottom line is that you don't trust me—that's it, isn't it?'

'Of course it's not,' she floundered.

'Then why have you never said you loved me?'

'Of course I have,' she protested. 'Dammit, I sleep with you, don't I?'

'But you've never once said you love me, Claire.'

It was true and she knew it, and because she didn't know what to say she took refuge in attack.

'I'm not a child, Jordan,' she said quickly. 'If this is your convoluted way of trying to tell me that you think you might have made a mistake, moving in with me, then I understand.'

He gazed heavenwards with exasperation and then swore, long and low and fluently.

'God almighty, woman, trying to pin you down is like trying to hold onto an eel! You know damn well that I don't want to leave, but I don't want to live with just half of you either.'

His eyes were fixed on her and she couldn't meet them.

'You're talking in riddles,' she muttered.

'Am I?' he said, clasping her tightly by the shoulders and forcing her to look up at him. 'Am I, really?'

'You are—you know you are,' she exclaimed.

'Then why have you never said you love me? Why, when I make love to you, do I always feel that there's a part of you that's not there?'

How did he know? she wondered. How could he possibly have guessed that even in their most intimate moments she kept a part of herself hidden from him?

'Jordan—'

'Answer me, Claire,' he broke in insistently. 'Why won't you say you love me?'

She opened her mouth and then closed it again and drew a ragged breath.

'Because…because I'm frightened,' she said, her voice breaking slightly. 'Because I said it to Max when we got married, and I meant it, Jordan—I really did mean it. I meant until death do us part. I meant forsaking all others, and within five years I knew that I didn't love him any more.'

'But it wouldn't be like that for us,' he declared vehemently.

'You don't know that,' she cried. 'Nobody does.'

He stared down at her for a long moment, and then he released her. 'I see.'

'Jordan, I'm sorry,' she murmured, her voice choked with unshed tears.

'Not half as sorry as I am,' he replied, turning on his heel.

'Where...where are you going?' she asked as a deep feeling of dread crept over her.

'Back to my flat. I'll collect my clothes and my books tomorrow.'

He went out of the sitting room and she ran after him.

'Jordan, you don't have to go. We can continue on like we were before, can't we?'

He came to a halt.

'No, we can't, Claire,' he said sadly, 'because I want all of you, not just the little bit you're prepared to give.'

'But I don't want you to go,' she protested. 'I want you to stay.'

His eyes held hers. 'Why, Claire?'

She knew what he wanted her to say. She knew that she had only to say those three little words and he would stay, but she couldn't say them.

'I'm...I'm sorry, Jordan,' she whispered instead.

'So am I,' he said as he opened the front door and went out, closing it quietly behind him.

For a long time she stood in the silent hallway, and as she slowly went along to the kitchen a small sob escaped from her.

'Oh, Anne,' she whispered. 'You were so wrong when you said getting involved with somebody again was worth the risk. It isn't worth it. It isn't worth it at all.'

CHAPTER NINE

'YOU'RE a very elusive man, Jordan.'

'And a busy one, Peter,' he replied, striding past him. 'I'm due in Theatre in fifteen minutes.'

'That's a shame, especially as I wanted to talk to you about Claire.'

Jordan came to a halt in the centre of the corridor.

'What about Claire?' he said, his brows lowering ominously.

'It's rather a delicate matter,' Peter observed, 'but if you don't mind talking in the corridor…'

Jordan stared at him for a moment and then pushed open the office door. 'In here.'

'But your secretary—'

'Roz has gone down to the lab to collect some reports,' Jordan cut in. 'She'll be back soon so make it quick.'

With a shrug Peter followed him into the office and went across to the window. Down in the car park he could see the gardeners, busily removing the dead daffodils from the ornamental tubs. He'd have to have a word with the landscape department, he decided with a frown. It didn't take three men to fill a few tubs with summer bedding plants.

'You said you wanted to talk to me about Claire,' Jordan said, breaking into his reverie. There was a decided edge to his voice and Peter turned towards him with a smile.

'Ah, yes. Our unpredictable head of department. I'm sure it will come as no great surprise to you that her temporary contract as head of department is not going to be made permanent.'

Jordan sat down on the edge of Roz's desk, his face impassive. 'Go on.'

'I've been instructed by the board to ask if you would consider accepting the position.'

'No.'

'It's a very good post, Jordan,' Peter observed. 'I doubt if you'd find a better one, and you told me yourself that you liked working here.'

'I do, but I won't accept a position at Claire's expense,' Jordan said firmly.

Peter nodded. 'A noble sentiment, but a pointless one. The post isn't—won't be—hers. I have a great admiration for Claire—'

'So I understand,' Jordan said through clenched teeth.

The colour on Peter's cheeks darkened momentarily but if he was wondering just how much Claire might have revealed about that unfortunate incident in her office he didn't appear inclined to ask.

'The problem is that if you don't accept the post then we'll have to offer it to somebody else,' he said instead. 'And then Claire might not have a job at all.'

Jordan stood up fast, his blue eyes cold. 'You can't sack her. You might be able to demote her but you can't sack her.'

'Of course we can't—and nor would we wish to,' Peter said with a smile, 'but do you honestly think that she would want to stay on here if someone from outside got her job?'

She wouldn't. Jordan knew without a shadow of a doubt that she wouldn't.

'Which is why we would like you to give very serious consideration to our offer before you refuse it,' Peter said. 'Claire is an excellent doctor, and we don't want to lose her. We feel that she might be persuaded to stay on if you were appointed rather than somebody else.'

Jordan gazed at him for a moment and then his lip curled. 'The bottom line is that you want Claire out—that's it, isn't it, Peter?'

'Surprisingly enough, I don't,' he replied. 'Look,' he continued as Jordan opened his mouth, clearly intending to protest. 'My job is to get the best possible people for the hospital and you're the best. In a few years time Claire would probably make an excellent head of department, but not right now. Right now she's more suited to being an assistant.'

'She wouldn't stay on if I got the job,' Jordan declared.

'I think you could persuade her,' Peter observed. 'I think you could be a very persuasive man if you wanted to be. And now I mustn't keep you.' He walked across to the office door and opened it. 'You said you were due in Theatre.'

Jordan followed him out into the corridor, a deep frown on his face.

'Peter—'

'Think about it, Jordan,' he cut in, 'but don't think too long. I need to know soon if you want the head of department's job or not.'

Something—a sound, or a flurry of movement—caught Jordan's attention and he turned quickly.

'What is it?' Peter asked, following the direction of his gaze.

A puzzled frown appeared on Jordan's forehead as he gazed down the empty corridor.

'Nothing,' he said slowly. 'I thought…just for a minute that I saw…but it's nothing.'

Peter nodded. 'I'll talk to you again, Jordan, but will you at least agree to think about my proposal? It's a good deal, believe me. You'll get what you want, we'll get what we want.'

'And Claire?' Jordan asked.

'Like I said, I'm sure you can be very persuasive when you want to be.'

He had been once, Jordan thought as he made for the stairs, but it had been a month now since he'd moved out of Claire's flat—a month that had seemed like a lifetime.

He missed her so much—and it wasn't just the feel of her body close to him at night. He missed her humour and her laughter. He missed sharing meals with her and talking over the day's events. And most of all he missed the glow that had once been in her slate-grey eyes when she'd looked at him.

Was it unreasonable of him to want her to tell him that she loved him? Sometimes he thought it was. Sometimes in the loneliness of the night he almost managed to persuade himself that it didn't matter if she said it or not, but he knew that it did.

'Bill's given Mrs Hunter her pre-med so we're ready to go whenever you are,' Debbie said as he swung through the doors of the changing room outside Theatre Two.

He nodded and went into one of the cubicles.

Claire had told him once that he kept too much of himself hidden—that he should reveal his feelings more—and she had been right. That was why his marriage had failed, and why every other relationship he'd had since had failed.

A bitter smile crossed his face as he began stripping off his clothes. This time he had made his feelings only too plain and yet he'd still managed to mess it up. Claire didn't want him in the way that he wanted her, and he couldn't settle for less.

'Are you ready to go, Jordan?' Debbie called.

'Just coming,' he shouted back, and heard the door to the changing room clatter shut.

And now, on top of everything else, he had Peter's offer to contend with.

Much as he hated to admit it, Peter was right about Claire. She wasn't ready to carry the full responsibility of a department yet, but if he accepted Peter's proposal she would never forgive him. And yet if he didn't accept it...

He sighed as he came out of the cubicle. 'You're stuck between a rock and a hard place, Jordan,' he murmured. 'And the only thing you can hope is that Claire doesn't ever find out about Peter's offer.'

Claire sighed as she stared out of her consulting room window, and the spring sunshine cast a warm glow onto her

face. It would soon be summer. Summer with its promise
of warm days and balmy nights, and yet all she could see,
stretching ahead of her, was an aching loneliness.

Wearily she leant her forehead against the glass and
closed her eyes. She wouldn't have believed that she could
have missed Jordan so much and yet she did. And it wasn't
just the comforting warmth of his arms around her in bed
at night that she missed. She missed the man himself.

Your flat's nice and neat again, a little voice whispered,
and a wry laugh escaped her. She would have given anything in the world—anything but the one thing he wanted—
to have his clothes and books scattered all over the place
again.

Her intercom buzzed and she stretched out to answer it.

'Mrs White for you, Claire.'

For a moment she didn't say anything and then she
straightened her back. 'Send her in, Roz.'

Gillian White looked as drained as she herself felt, and
Claire smiled sympathetically at her.

'How have you been keeping, Gillian?'

'OK, I guess.'

'And your husband?'

The girl shrugged. 'Fine.'

Claire gave her a searching gaze and then flicked open
her file. 'It's been a month since your operation, and what
I'd like to do today is discuss where we go from here.'

Gillian said nothing and Claire closed the file quickly.

'Do you want to stop the treatment, Gillian? If you don't
want to go on with it you only have to say so.'

Gillian stared down at her hands and her voice was
choked with unshed tears. 'My husband wants me to stop.
He said he almost lost me the last time and no baby is
worth it.'

'And you—what do you think?' Claire asked gently.

'I don't want to stop. I want to keep on trying until I
have a baby.'

'But, Gillian, if your husband doesn't want you to continue—'

'It's not his decision,' she said vehemently. 'He doesn't have to do anything. It's me who has to take the drugs, me who has to go through all the treatment. I want to carry on.'

Claire sighed. She wasn't happy about this, but Gillian's infertility treatment wasn't like IVF. The law didn't require her to get both partners' consent.

'Look, I'd really like to talk to your husband first,' she said. 'I've got a spare hour next Thursday—could the two of you come in then and we can talk about it?'

'But—'

'Gillian, your husband clearly loves you very much. Is it really worth having a baby if you lose him in the process?'

'I won't.'

'You might,' Claire insisted. 'Men have feelings, too, and if he feels that you're shutting him out you could end up with no marriage.'

Gillian bit her lip. 'I'll ask him to come in, but he's not going to make me change my mind. No matter what he says, he's not going to make me change my mind.'

Claire stared into space for a long time after Gillian had left. She had told her that she was shutting her husband out, forgetting that he had feelings, too, but wasn't that exactly what she'd done to Jordan?

He'd said that she'd been using him, giving him only a part of herself. He'd been right, but she'd been afraid of letting herself fall in love again.

So afraid, she suddenly realised, that without even knowing it she had actually allowed Max to go on hurting her. He hadn't been hurt by the divorce. He had made a new life for himself but she hadn't. She'd withdrawn into herself, letting her failed marriage sour her attitude towards any other relationship.

Could she change? She knew that she wanted to, but could she?

The intercom on her desk buzzed and she answered it with a sigh.

'You haven't forgotten that you're supposed to be doing Mrs Gordon's op at four, have you?' Roz said tactfully.

Claire's eyes flew to the clock. She had forgotten—totally and completely forgotten—and the worst of it was that Mr Kennedy had arranged for one of his students to watch her operate.

With a muttered oath she flew out of her room and down the stairs to the theatre.

'I'm sorry I'm a bit late—Beth, isn't it?' she exclaimed as soon as she saw the student. 'I had a bit of an emergency upstairs.'

The girl nodded understandingly. 'It's OK, Dr Fraser. Jordan made sure I wasn't bored.'

Claire's eyebrows rose slightly. 'Jordan?'

Beth blushed. 'He told me to call him that. He said all of the staff at the Ravelston call him by his first name.'

They did, but that didn't mean that Claire had to like the idea of this tall, willowy girl with her mass of blonde hair doing it too.

'And how—exactly—did Jordan make sure that you weren't bored?' she asked, with a slight edge to her voice as she got into her theatre clothes.

'Well, I arrived a bit early and he asked if I'd like to watch him perform a fimbrioplasty.'

'I hope you didn't get in his way,' Claire said with concern. 'It's quite a tricky business, reconstructing the end of a Fallopian tube once the blockage has been removed.'

'He didn't seem to mind me being there.' Beth laughed, revealing a row of perfect white teeth. 'In fact, he said it was a pleasure to have such pretty company.'

'Did he?' Claire replied dryly. 'Well, I'm afraid Mrs Gordon's endometriosis isn't going to be nearly so thrilling, but it will be good experience for you if you intend to specialise in infertility treatment.'

'Oh, I do,' Beth breathed. 'I can think of nothing I'd like better than to work with Jordan—and with you, too, of course, Dr Fraser.'

Oh, I'll just bet you would, Claire thought, pulling on her surgical gloves with a snap.

'What can you tell me about endometriosis?' she asked, as they went into the operating theatre to find Mrs Gordon already deep under the anaesthetic.

Beth frowned. 'For some reason it's most commonly found amongst British and American women. Did you know that Jordan worked in America for ten years, Dr Fraser?'

'Yes, I did,' Claire answered in a clipped tone. 'So, instead of regaling me with details of Dr Marshall's private life, perhaps you'd care to tell me what else you know about endometriosis.'

The girl blinked and Claire bit her lip behind her mask. She knew she was behaving like a bitch, but something about the student doctor's youthful enthusiasm for Jordan was getting under her skin.

'It's an odd condition,' Beth observed. 'The lining of the uterus doesn't just grow where it should. It can also grow around the ovaries, the tubes and sometimes even the outer linings of the pelvic organs.'

Quickly Claire made two incisions into Mrs Gordon's abdomen. 'And what sort of damage does this extraneous lining do?'

'If it's around the tubes it can cause adhesions or scarring. It doesn't usually cause infertility so I'd guess that in Mrs Gordon's case it must be interfering in some way with her ovulation.'

She was bright as well as pretty, Claire thought with irritation. No wonder Jordan had enjoyed talking to her.

'Symptoms of endometriosis?' she asked, hoping to catch the girl out, but, of course, she didn't.

'Painful or heavy, irregular periods. Of course, lots of women suffer from that,' Beth added, 'so it's not a cast-iron diagnosis. The safest way to know for sure is to perform a laparoscopy.'

Smart alec, Claire thought sourly, and then was angry with herself for her reaction. Beth was bright and keen—in fact, she was exactly the type she should be encouraging to go into infertility treatment—and yet she was biting the girl's head off at every opportunity.

Swiftly she inserted a fine metal electrode into Mrs Gordon's abdomen and then eased the laparoscope into place.

'Jordan said that in cases of bad endometriosis it was better to use microsurgery to remove it,' Beth observed, watching her.

'He's quite correct,' Claire replied evenly. 'Luckily, Mrs Gordon's condition doesn't warrant that, but if it had I would have tried to cut away the islands and then divide the adhesions.'

'Jordan said that it's a very difficult operation.'

'Jordan appears to have had rather a lot to say while he was performing Mrs Hunter's fimbrioplasty,' Claire said with a calmness that was deceptive, and heard Beth laugh.

'Oh, he does like to talk—and he's such a fascinating man, isn't he?'

Claire peered down the laparoscope and then manoeuvred the electrode onto the little islands of endometrium. Once she was certain it was in place she passed an electrical current through the islands to burn them out—and wished with all her heart that she was burning the student doctor's long blonde hair instead.

She was jealous. No matter much how she tried to persuade herself otherwise, she knew that she was jealous of the girl standing opposite her—and she also knew why. Despite all her resolve—despite all her vows that she would never put her heart on the line again—she had fallen in love with Jordan Marshall.

'But is that possible, Dr Fraser?'

She looked up, red-cheeked, to see Beth, regarding her thoughtfully.

Dear God, surely she hadn't spoken out loud?

'Is what possible, Beth?' she hedged.

'That you can still get pregnant even if you have very bad endometriosis?'

'Of course it is,' Claire answered with relief. 'And once you're pregnant it doesn't affect the baby, nor is there any statistical proof that it increases the risk of a miscarriage or an ectopic pregnancy.'

Quickly she finished burning the last of the islands and then removed the electrode and the laparoscope.

'Would you like to suture for me?'

'May I?' Beth exclaimed in delight. 'Jordan wouldn't let me do it for Mrs Hunter. He said it was too tricky. But he did say that if he ever needed a pretty assistant he'd be sure to send for me,' she added with a chuckle. 'He's a real charmer, isn't he?'

Well, he's not going to charm you, Claire thought determinedly.

With the operation over, and Mrs Gordon happily recovering under Debbie's watchful eye, Claire swiftly changed back into her ordinary clothes.

'This afternoon's been really interesting, Dr Fraser,' Beth said as she watched Claire drag a brush through her hair and then apply a touch of lipstick. 'Would it be OK if I asked Mr Kennedy if I can come again?'

'We're really busy just now,' Claire lied. 'Maybe in a couple of weeks?'

Beth nodded, disappointment on her pretty face, as Claire dashed out of the changing room and made for the stairs.

The last thing she wanted was to have the girl hanging around Jordan. She wanted him for herself and if it wasn't too late she was going to have him.

She had just reached the top of the stairs, however, when she saw Alan and Helen Elliot, walking down the corridor, and from the smiles on the couple's faces they had just been given some good news.

'I'm pregnant, Dr Fraser,' Helen exclaimed. 'I'm actually four weeks pregnant!'

'That's marvellous,' Claire smiled. 'Congratulations to you both.'

Alan Elliot beamed. 'We're just off to phone the family to give them the good news.'

'I hope everything goes well for you—I really do,' Claire declared and Helen laughed.

'You should try it some time, Doctor—being pregnant, I mean!'

Maybe she would, Claire thought as she watched the couple making for the lift. Max had always wanted children but she'd said that she'd wanted to wait a while. What she'd really meant, of course, was that she'd been too interested in furthering her career to want to take time out to have a family. But it was different now, very different.

'You've just made two people very happy,' she said to Jordan as he appeared at the end of the corridor.

'That's one I've been able to win, anyway,' he said cryptically.

She flushed. 'Jordan…'

He didn't even look at her. He just strode past her into his room and shut the door, leaving her standing outside.

She sighed. He clearly wasn't going to make this easy for her but, then, why should he? She'd treated him badly and it was up to her to make the first move.

She took a deep breath and tapped on the door.

'Something I can help you with?' he said as she opened it.

Never had he looked so unapproachable. Surely she hadn't left it too late? Painfully conscious that it was her own stupid fault if she had left it too late, she swallowed hard.

'Jordan, I…I'd like you to come back.'

'Come back?' he repeated, with a slight frown.

'Move back in with me—come and live with me again.'

He stared at the sheet of papers in his hand. 'Why?'

He definitely wasn't going to make this easy for her, she realised, and she took an uncertain step forward.

'Because…because I miss you.'

'Buy a hot-water bottle. That should keep you warm on cold nights.'

She flushed scarlet. 'Jordan—'

'I'm busy, Claire,' he said abruptly, 'so if there's nothing else…?'

Her throat was so tight it hurt, but she knew she couldn't just leave it like this. If there was even the remotest chance that he might still love her then she had to find out.

'Jordan.'

'Mmm?' he said vaguely, his eyes fixed on the notes in his hand.

'I…I love you,' she whispered.

His head didn't come up but she thought he stiffened.

'I'm sorry, I didn't quite catch that,' he murmured.

She took another step forward. 'I said I love you, Jordan.'

He put one finger against his ear and rubbed it vigorously. 'Sorry, but I didn't quite get that either.'

She stared down at him in confusion and just for an instant she saw the corners of his mouth curve upwards. A ripple of laughter bubbled inside her and she reached across his desk, whisked the papers out of his hand and hit him over the head with them.

'You rat—you heard me the first time, didn't you?'

'Of course I did,' he said with a grin, 'but I'm superstitious. I reckon you have to say a thing three times before it's true.'

'I've only said it twice,' she pointed out.

'I know,' he said huskily, putting his hands up to clasp her wrists. 'Want to go for broke?'

She bent her head and brushed his lips gently with her own. 'I love you, Jordan Marshall.'

He sprang to his feet and let out such a yell that the windows in his consulting room rattled.

'You're pleased?' She laughed as he caught her by the waist and whirled her around.

'Pleased—*pleased*?' he gasped. 'Oh, Claire—'

'Will you move back into my place tonight?' she said breathlessly as he showered her face with kisses.

'Books, clothes, the lot,' he exclaimed. 'When are you going to marry me?'

'One thing at a time, Jordan,' she protested.

'*When*, Claire?' he demanded, and she smiled.

'Whenever you want.'

He crushed her to him.

'You've no idea how much I've missed you,' he said into her throat. 'Let's go home.'

'Home?' she echoed.

'It's five o'clock, I'm finished for the day and you've no more patients.'

'But I've got a pile of paperwork to catch up on—'

'Leave it,' he interrupted.

'I can't.'

'Yes, you can,' he said firmly, 'because if you don't...'

'You'll do what?' she asked provocatively, and saw his eyes sparkle.

'I'll rip off all your clothes and make mad, passionate love to you right here and now on the floor.'

She put her head to one side, as though considering his proposal seriously, and then shook her head.

'We'd better go home. I don't think the cleaners would appreciate it if they had to vacuum around us.'

He threw back his head and laughed, and she made for the door.

'Just give me five minutes to collect my bag and lock up my room,' she continued. 'And then I'm all yours.'

'Five minutes, Claire,' he called after her, 'but that's all. If you're any longer I'll carry you out over my shoulder.'

He could hear her laughing as she went down the corridor, and a broad grin appeared on his face.

Never had he felt this happy. He wanted to throw open his window and shout his delight to the world. He wanted to marry her right now, this very minute, so that she would be his always.

His smile deepened as he put the Elliots' file into his filing cabinet. He hoped Claire wanted children. Girls, he decided as he went over to his desk and locked it. He wanted them all to be girls, each and every one a pint-sized edition of their mother.

He hung up his white coat and then frowned slightly. She was taking a lot longer than five minutes to pick up her bag and lock up. Knowing her, she'd probably got waylaid by a telephone call. Well, he wasn't going to allow her to be waylaid, not tonight.

Whistling cheerfully, he went out along the corridor to her room.

'Claire, how do you feel about children?' he asked as he opened her door. 'I quite fancy having a few myself...'

He came to a halt. She was staring down at her desk, her face chalk-white, and he took a step forward with concern.

'Are you OK?'

'You just missed Anne Sommerville.'

Her voice sounded odd, tight, and his eyebrows rose. 'Something wrong in ICBU?'

'Not in ICBU, no.'

There was a stillness about her that was unnerving, an emptiness in her grey eyes as she looked at him that made his stomach suddenly contract.

'What's wrong, Claire?'

'Anne came up to see me earlier today,' she said slowly. 'She'd managed to get tickets for the concert at the King's Theatre on Saturday and wanted to know if I'd like to go. She didn't see me—I had a patient with me at the time— but she did see you. You were talking to Peter Thornton.'

His lips felt suddenly dry and he ran his tongue over them nervously.

'So?' he said, though he had a dreadful feeling that he knew what was coming next.

'She heard Peter offer you my job.'

He swallowed. So he'd been right—there *had* been somebody in the corridor.

'Claire, it's not what you think—'

'Then how come you know what I'm thinking?' she countered, her voice bitter. 'That day when you took me to work on the back of your motorbike and those businessmen saw me. That morning when Peter and the board members walked in on us in the changing room. You really worked hard to discredit me, didn't you, Jordan?'

He coloured. 'Claire, those were complete accidents—'

'And sleeping with me—was that a complete accident too?' she interrupted, her grey eyes cold. 'And moving in with me—was that another accident or were you just hoping to find out more about me so that you could dish the dirt later?'

'Claire, I didn't sleep with you because I wanted your job,' he protested. 'I slept with you because I loved you— I still do.'

'I think "wanted" might be closer to the truth,' she replied, her lip curling slightly. 'And I suppose I shouldn't really blame you. Every ambitious man should have some recreation, and you managed to combine business with pleasure—very convenient.'

'Claire.'

'How do you manage to sleep nights, Jordan—or does stabbing people in the back get easier after you've done it a few times?'

'Claire, it isn't like that—'

Her eyebrows rose. 'No? Then tell me what it's like— I'd be interested to hear.'

He didn't want to tell her, but he knew there was no other way.

'Claire, the board was never going to make your contract permanent.'

'That's not true,' she flared. 'They would have done it if you hadn't come along, deliberately making me look ridiculous, unprofessional—'

'They wouldn't,' he interrupted gently. 'It was never a possibility.'

She got to her feet angrily. 'You're lying—I know you are.'

'I'm not,' he said tersely. 'Claire, the truth is that you don't have enough experience to run the department. You're a skilled doctor and an excellent surgeon, but I'm six years older than you. I've got the experience you lack, and that's why the hospital wants me.'

Was it true? she wondered as she stared back at him. Had the board never intended to make her appointment permanent? Suddenly she remembered the brass name-plate that had been on Jordan's consulting-room door the day he'd arrived. Peter would never have allowed that kind of expense for a man who was only going to stay at the hospital for a year. So it was true. All those hours she'd put in, all that work she'd done, had been for nothing.

'What did you tell Peter?' she asked, her voice low.

His colour deepened. 'That I'd think about it.'

'What's there to think about?' she said with an effort. 'It's a good job. And I ought to know, it used to be mine.'

'I'll only take the job if you agree to be my assistant,' he said softly.

'And have everybody at the hospital know that I'd been demoted?' she said, her voice bitter. 'Have everyone wonder whether I'd slept with you to get it?'

'They wouldn't think that,' he insisted. 'Claire, I know you're angry right now, and you've every right to be—'

'How long have you known that the board wasn't going to make my post permanent, Jordan?' she interrupted suddenly.

He tried to meet her gaze, and couldn't. 'A little while.'

'How long, Jordan?' she demanded, her face taut.

'Since just before Christmas,' he muttered.

'And this is the beginning of May. How long were you going to wait before you told me, Jordan? The day before my contract ran out?'

'Claire, I wanted to tell you,' he exclaimed, 'but I didn't want to hurt you.'

'And how do you think I feel right now?' she asked, her grey eyes blank. 'Knowing that you've lied to me...'

'I didn't lie to you,' he protested.

'Maybe not in words, but you knew what was going on and yet you didn't tell me,' she said. 'You knew how important this job was to me, and yet you let me go on believing that it was going to be mine when all the time you knew that it wasn't. How many other lies have you told me, Jordan?'

He strode across the room and clutched her hands tightly in his.

'None. Claire, I love you. Tell me what I've got to say to make it right.'

She pulled her hands free from his grasp. 'I think goodbye would just about cover it.'

'Claire.'

'I'm going home, Jordan.'

'But, Claire—'

'I'm going home, and when I see you again tomorrow this subject is closed, OK?'

She made for the door and he caught hold of her arm. 'Claire, I want to marry you.'

She pulled her arm free from him with such a look of loathing that he stepped back from her quickly.

'I wouldn't marry you if you were the last man on God's earth, Jordan!'

'Claire, listen to me. I know what you must think of me right now—'

'Oh, no,' she broke in, her voice trembling. 'I don't think

you could even begin to imagine what I think of you right now.' And she pushed past him out of the door.

How could she have been so stupid? she wondered as she ran down the stairs and out into the car park. How could she not have seen that Jordan was a taker and a user?

She should have realised. All those patients who had suddenly wanted to change doctors, all those times he had said he wanted to help her. He hadn't wanted to help her—he had wanted to help himself.

Wretchedly she got into her car and slammed the door.

Maybe he's telling the truth, a small voice whispered, maybe he really does love you.

A tear ran down her cheek and angrily she wiped it away with her sleeve. Even if he did love her, how could she ever trust him again? He had lied once—how could she be sure that he wouldn't do it again?

A tap on her window made her jump and she rolled it down to see Andy, the car-park attendant, regarding her curiously.

'Are you OK, Dr Fraser?' he asked.

'I'm fine, just fine,' she said with difficulty. 'Today...today's just been a bad day, that's all.'

He nodded sympathetically. 'Sometimes life's a bummer, isn't it, Doc?'

She smiled back at him through a blur of tears and nodded. 'Yes, Andy,' she murmured. 'Sometimes life's a bummer.'

CHAPTER TEN

'But this is such a shock, Claire.'

'Really, Peter?' she replied dryly. 'I'd have thought you'd have considered it more of a pleasure to receive my resignation.'

Peter looked hurt. 'Of course I don't. You're an excellent doctor and the very last thing we want is to lose you.'

'Keep that up and I might change my mind,' she said, and then laughed. 'Don't look so worried, Peter, I won't.'

'Now, really, Claire—'

'According to my contract, I should give you three months' notice,' she went on, 'but if you'll take my six weeks' holiday leave into account I could be out of your hair by the beginning of August.'

He glanced at his calendar. 'It's not really an ideal time, what with holidays coming up—'

'I'm sure you and Dr Marshall will manage,' she said, getting to her feet.

'Does Jordan know about this?'

'No, and I don't see why he has to—at least not yet,' she said firmly.

Peter sighed and shook his head. 'It's your decision, Claire. I'd like to say that I think it's a great pity you're leaving us—'

'But you won't,' she broke in, 'because I don't think that even you're that big a hypocrite, Peter.'

She swept out of the door, her back straight and her head held high, feeling relief after the weeks of uncertainty. Behind her, a broad smile appeared on Peter Thornton's face as he reached for his phone.

*   *   *

'You'll have to tell Jordan soon,' Anne said, leaning back in her seat, her brown eyes troubled.

'I know.'

'And if you don't tell him you're most definitely going to have to tell Roz,' Anne continued. 'You've only got another month before you leave, and you can't abandon her to cope with a stack of cancelled appointments.'

'I know, I know!' Claire exclaimed irritably.

Anne looked at her thoughtfully for a moment. 'I still don't understand why you're leaving at all. You told me yourself that you were finding it really hard, running your department. If you accepted the post as Jordan's assistant, all the pressure would be off you and you could just get on with your job.'

'Knowing that everyone was sniggering about me behind my back, saying I wasn't up to the top job?' Claire shook her head. 'No, thanks.'

Anne stared down for a moment and then cleared her throat tentatively.

'What if Jordan really does love you?'

'He doesn't,' Claire said tightly. 'And if he does, it's the kind of warped love that I can do without.'

Anne shook her head. 'I wish I hadn't told you what I overheard. You were so happy.'

'I was living in a fool's paradise,' Claire said. 'You did me a favour, believe me.'

'But—'

'He lied to me, Anne.'

'It wasn't exactly a lie—more a withholding of information.'

'There's a difference?'

'Yes, there is—if he really does love you.'

'Well, I don't love him.'

Anne's eyebrows rose. 'No? Claire, are you sure it's not just your pride that's hurt—because he was offered the job and you weren't?'

'Of course my pride's hurt!'

'And I understand that,' Anne observed, 'but I never thought I'd see the day when you'd care more about what people thought than about your own happiness.'

Claire opened her mouth, then closed it again and got to her feet.

'Oh...go boil your head, Anne!' she retorted.

She heard Anne starting to laugh as she went out of ICBU and she could still hear her laughing when she reached the stairs.

Anne didn't know what she was talking about, she thought savagely. How would she like it if someone joined her department, made love to her and then got her job? OK, so maybe she did care too much about what other people thought, but pride was the only thing she'd had left after her divorce, pride in her abilities and her work—and Jordan had taken that away.

'Dr Fraser!'

It was the Hardings, coming out of Jordan's room, and quickly she fixed a smile to her lips.

'Today's the big day, Doctor,' Liz declared, holding up her nasal spray. 'We're just starting on our second course of IVF.'

'I'll keep my fingers crossed for you that it works,' Claire replied.

But I'm never going to know how it turns out, she thought with a sigh as she watched the couple walk to the lift. And she wanted to know.

She wanted to know about so many of their patients: Gillian White, who had finally persuaded her husband to agree to her carrying on with her treatment; Mary Bell, who was twenty-seven weeks pregnant; Helen Elliot, who was twelve weeks pregnant, and so many others she'd seen through the good times and the bad.

'Claire.'

She stiffened and dug her fists deep into the pockets of her white coat.

'Something I can do for you, Jordan?' she asked evenly,
turning to face him.

'Claire, please,' he said, his face tired. 'You won't answer my phone calls, you ignore me at work, you shut the
door in my face when I come to your flat—'

'What did you expect?' she interrupted, her grey eyes
flashing. 'Did you expect me just to forgive you?'

He shook his head. 'I didn't expect it, but I hoped after
you'd had time to calm down—'

'Oh, I've calmed down now,' she said tightly. 'I see
everything very clearly now.'

'Claire, please—'

'No, Jordan,' she broke in sharply. 'No more excuses,
no more lies. Whatever we had is finished.' And without a
backward glance she walked away from him into Roz's
office.

'Does Jordan know about this?' her secretary asked some
minutes later when Claire had told her that she was leaving.

'God in heaven, why does everybody ask me that?'
Claire exclaimed. 'What I do—or don't do—is none of his
business.'

'You've had a row, haven't you?' Roz said shrewdly.
'Honestly, Claire, this relationship of yours is on and off
more often than an electric light bulb.'

'Dr Marshall and I do not have a relationship,' Claire
replied through gritted teeth. 'We have never had a relationship and we never will.'

'OK, OK, I get the picture,' her secretary exclaimed, putting her hands up in a gesture of defeat. 'But he isn't going
to like it.'

I hope he doesn't, Claire thought as she made her way
to her room. I hope he's miserable as hell. I hope that when
Peter makes him head of department he chokes on it.

She banged into her room and threw herself down on her
seat. Four more weeks. How on earth was she going to
endure four more weeks of this? She should have told Peter
that she was leaving immediately but she knew she could

never have done that. No matter how angry she might be with Jordan she could never just have abandoned her patients.

Quickly she opened her desk and pulled out an armful of files. Work, that was the best medicine. She would make a start on deciding which patients could have their appointments cancelled, but after an hour and a half she had little to show for her efforts, apart from the beginnings of a pounding headache.

Coffee, she decided. A good strong cup of coffee was what she needed, but just as she reached the door her intercom buzzed. For a moment she considered ignoring it but she knew that she couldn't, and with a deep sigh she leant across the desk and pushed the button.

'Claire—my room—*now*!' Jordan said urgently. 'Mary Bell's here and it looks as though she's gone into labour!'

She was out of the door before he had even finished speaking, and when she flew into his room she found Mary on the examination couch, looking absolutely terrified. Her husband was kneeling beside her, his face white and drawn.

'Are you sure, Jordan?' she gasped breathlessly. 'It couldn't just be an antepartum haemorrhage?'

'It may be more years than I care to remember since I assisted at a birth,' he replied ruefully, 'but I think even I can recognise the signs.'

'Sorry,' she said, equally rueful. 'What happened?'

'She just popped in to say hello and her waters broke in the lift.'

'Shall I call Maternity?' she said, and reached for the phone, only to see Jordan shake his head.

'It's too late. Her cervix has already dilated to ten centimetres and the contractions are coming every few minutes.'

'Oh, hell,' she muttered.

'Exactly,' he agreed. 'It looks like we're going into the maternity business whether we like it or not.'

Quickly she pressed his intercom. 'Roz, phone Anne

Sommerville and tell her we need an incubator now. We've got a baby on the way.'

An amazed squeak came from Roz, then the intercom went dead. Claire fixed an encouraging smile to her face.

'I thought I told you that we didn't deal with births?' she chastised as she gently felt Mary's abdomen. 'What are you trying to do—make a liar out of me?'

'Oh, Doctor, I'm not going to lose the baby, am I?' she replied tearfully. 'I've got so far…'

'Everything will be fine, I'm sure,' Claire said soothingly.

'But she's only twenty-seven weeks!' Richard Bell exclaimed.

It was close, but babies born at that age could survive if they were put into an incubator quickly enough.

'Dr Marshall, I don't know what to do,' Mary sobbed, clutching at his hand wildly. 'The childbirth classes don't start until next week.'

'Hey, trust me.' He smiled encouragingly, and Claire felt as though a knife had twisted in her heart.

That's what she'd done once—trusted him—and all it had brought her were heartache and pain.

'OK, Mary, I want you to push when I tell you to push, and relax when I tell you to relax,' she said quickly, banishing her thoughts to the back of her mind. 'Now huff, puff and push!'

Mary did as instructed and let out a groan.

'You're doing fine, just fine,' Claire said. 'Now relax for a minute and then—'

She came to a halt as Jordan's consulting-room door banged open and Anne Sommerville appeared, wheeling an incubator.

'I know you specialise in infertility treatments, Claire, but this is ridiculous,' she said with a grin as some of her nurses appeared behind her.

'It wasn't planned, I can assure you.' She smiled back. 'OK, Mary, push again, push really hard.'

'Can't you give her something—a painkiller of some sort?' Richard Bell said, wiping his forehead with his handkerchief as his wife let out a cry that was halfway between a scream and a groan.

Claire shook her head. 'By the time it worked the baby would be here.'

'It's that close?' he gasped.

She nodded. 'It's that close. Now, relax, Mary, relax, and push—push again!'

'The head's out,' Jordan murmured, reaching forward to support it.

'You're almost there, Mary,' Claire said encouragingly. 'Another push—a really big one. What on earth—?' she added, startled, as she heard a loud clatter behind her.

Jordan grinned. 'Our father-to-be just fainted.'

She shook her head and chuckled. 'OK, Mary, you're doing marvellously. A couple more pushes—that's all it needs.'

'But I can't, I can't!' she protested, sweat pouring down her face.

'Yes, you can. Relax, relax, now push, push— Oh, wonderful!'

With a tiny wail of protest the little boy slipped out into Jordan's hands. Quickly he clamped the umbilical cord and cut it.

'Ours now, I think,' Anne exclaimed, taking the child quickly but tenderly out of Jordan's hands and into the incubator.

'Is it all right—is my baby all right?' Mary gasped as the afterbirth came away.

'He's here and he's alive,' Jordan said softly as Anne and her team disappeared out of the door with their precious cargo. 'Our intensive care baby unit is one of the best in the world, Mary, and if anyone can pull him through they will.'

'It's a boy?' she said breathlessly. 'Richard, did you hear that—we've got a son.'

'I'm afraid your husband is otherwise engaged at the moment,' Claire said with amusement as Richard Bell was wheeled out on a trolley by one of the nurses from ICBU.

'Can I see my baby?' Mary begged as Jordan gently massaged her stomach to help control the blood flow.

He shook his head. 'The ICBU people will need to get him attached to a life-support machine first, but I'm sure you'll be able to see him soon.'

'This is all highly irregular,' a strident voice declared, and Claire turned to see the forceful figure of Sister Breton from Maternity standing in the doorway.

'And this room is getting to be like Piccadilly Circus,' Jordan muttered under his breath.

Claire choked down the laugh that sprang to her lips. 'Irregular but unavoidable, I'm afraid, Sister.'

'Well, you can leave it to the professionals now.' Sister Breton sniffed disapprovingly as two of her nurses gently eased Mary onto a trolley.

'Thank you, thank you both,' Mary whispered, reaching out to clasp both Jordan and Claire by the hand. 'I don't know what I'd have done without you.'

'Just don't make a habit of it, OK?' Claire smiled.

'Looks like you're going to need some cleaners, Jordan,' Roz observed as the room began to empty. 'I'll organise it for you right away.'

She was going to miss Roz, Claire thought as the girl bustled away. Nothing ruffled her, nothing threw her into a flap. She'd be very lucky to get someone as capable in her next job.

Her next job. She glanced up at Jordan. If it hadn't been for him, maybe she wouldn't be looking for her next job.

'Roz told me that you've resigned,' he said, as though he'd read her thoughts.

That was quick, she thought, even for her secretary.

'Money or a holiday in the sun would be nice,' she mused. 'If you're planning on a whip-round for my going-away present,' she continued as he stared at her in confusion, 'that's what I'd like.'

'You don't have to go,' he said quietly. 'My contract is up in a couple of months, and I won't take the head of department's job unless you agree to stay on as my assistant.'

'I have no intention of staying on,' she declared, her voice ice-cold. 'I'm leaving, and that's all there is to it.'

'Claire, can't we at least talk?' he begged.

'I don't think you would have anything to say that I would find even remotely interesting,' she said crisply, and walked out of the door.

The rest of the day seemed endless. Anne phoned from ICBU to say that Mary Bell's son was stable, and Maternity called to tell her that Mary was doing well and Richard had recovered sufficiently to go home.

Claire laughed when she put down the phone but her laughter quickly faded.

She was so tired, so very tired. Every day seemed interminable, every night never-ending as she tossed and turned sleeplessly. If only it were August now. If only she could just walk out of the Ravelston and never come back.

Her intercom buzzed and she answered it wearily.

'Sorry to bother you,' Roz said, 'but Mr and Mrs Elliot are here and they'd like a word with you, if you can spare the time.'

For a second she hesitated, knowing that she didn't want to see anybody at the moment, and then she sighed.

'Send them in.'

Helen and Alan Elliot came in, wreathed in smiles.

'No need to ask how you're feeling,' Claire exclaimed as she pulled two seats forward for the couple.

'Happy doesn't even come halfway to summing up how we feel, does it, love?' Helen declared, beaming at her husband.

'We were hoping to see both you and Dr Marshall today,' Alan Elliot said awkwardly. 'We've been transferred to Maternity, you see, and we wanted to thank you both for all that you've done for us.'

'I'm afraid he's got patients with him right now,' Claire began, 'but if you'd like to wait—'

'I'm afraid we can't,' Helen interjected. 'We'll see him another time, but Alan and I would like to give you something.'

Her husband dived into the shopping bag at his feet. 'We didn't know whether you were allowed to receive gifts or not,' he said, 'but we'd very much like you to accept this.'

It was a bottle of champagne, and Claire took it from him with surprise.

'It's by way of an apology, Doctor,' Alan continued awkwardly. 'I said a lot of things to you that I shouldn't when you told me about my poor sperm results and—'

'Forget it,' Claire said quickly. 'We all say a lot of things we don't mean in the heat of the moment.'

She had said a lot of things to Jordan that she hadn't meant because she had been so angry, she thought as the couple left.

Then take them back, her heart whispered. Go and see him, tell him you're sorry—that you overreacted. But people will talk, her mind argued. If you and Jordan become lovers again, people will say that's why you got the assistant head of department's job. That you couldn't cope with the top job, but you slept with the boss to get the assistant's position.

Unconsciously she shook her head. She couldn't do it, she just couldn't.

'Claire, you are never going to believe this,' Roz exclaimed, as she flew into the room, without knocking, 'but Jordan's down in A and E under security guard!'

'You're right—I don't believe it,' Claire replied, bending to retrieve the papers that had fluttered to the floor at Roz's entrance.

'But it's true!' her secretary protested. 'He hit Peter Thornton!'

Claire gazed at her blankly and then shook her head. 'You must have heard it wrong.'

'I didn't!' Roz gasped. 'You know how Peter's usual secretary's got the flu so they've got a temp, standing in for her?'

'Yes, but I don't see what that's got to do with—'

'Apparently, Jordan demanded to see Peter and although the new girl didn't recognise him, she let him go in. Suddenly she heard this almighty crash. She ran in, found Peter lying unconscious on the floor, with Jordan standing over him, thought she had an escaped lunatic on her hands and—'

'Phoned Security,' Claire finished for her with a groan. 'The idiot! Where is he now?'

'In A and E, being patched up.'

'Not Peter—Jordan.'

'I'm talking about Jordan. Apparently, the security guards got a bit enthusiastic when the temp told them Jordan had gone berserk.'

'What do you mean, they "got a bit enthusiastic"?' Claire asked, concern creeping over her.

Roz shook her head helplessly. 'All I know is that A and E have sent out for more B-type blood—'

Claire didn't wait to hear any more. She was out of the door and running.

It was only when she reached A and E that she wondered why on earth she had come. Just this morning she'd told herself that if she never saw Jordan again it would be too soon, that she hoped he would suffer when he was head of department. Well, that's why I'm here, she told herself, to see him suffer, but she knew it wasn't true.

'How is he, Marian?' she asked, recognising the staff nurse on duty.

'He's got a broken nose, and his dignity's taken a bit of a dent—'

'I meant Jordan,' Claire interrupted. 'How's Jordan?'

'Apart from having a lovely black eye, and being black and blue all over, he seems fine.'

'Then why did you need to send out for more blood?' Claire asked, bewildered.

'More blood?' Marian repeated. 'But that wasn't for Jordan. We've got a bad RTA due in at any minute. He is OK, Claire,' she continued gently, gazing at her with under-standing. 'In fact, he's the hero of the hour.'

'He's what?' Claire gasped, and saw Marian laugh.

'There's not a woman in the Ravelston who hasn't wanted to hit Peter at one time or another, Claire.'

'That's as may be, but—'

'Dr Fraser, I'm really sorry about this,' a voice said be-hind her, and Claire turned to see one of the security guards, regarding her uncomfortably. 'I didn't realise he worked for you, and when Charlie and me found Mr Thornton lying on the floor in his office...'

'It's OK,' she sighed. 'I know you were only doing your job.'

'He packs a real nifty right hook for a doctor,' the guard observed appreciatively. 'You know, if he were only ten years younger he could have a real future in the boxing ring.'

'By the time I get through with him, he'll be lucky if he can lift a stethoscope,' she said grimly. 'Where is he, Marian?'

'Cubicle five,' she replied. 'And go easy on him, Claire. He's feeling a bit fragile at the moment.'

Fragile! She'd give him fragile, Claire thought as she made her way down to the cubicle.

'Come to visit a dying man, have you?' Jordan said plaintively, as she pulled back the curtains and then closed them firmly again behind her.

'Come to add to his injuries, more like,' she snapped, secretly relieved to see that, although his left eye was half-closed, and his bare chest was a mass of bruises, he didn't appear badly hurt. 'What the hell got into you, hitting Peter like that for no reason?'

'I did have a reason,' he said. 'He made you resign.'

'And that's why you hit him?' she gasped. 'Because I resigned?'

'Partly,' he said ruefully. 'I tried to make him see sense, to tell him that he mustn't accept your resignation, but he wouldn't listen. Then I remembered what you told me— about him groping you—and I guess, well, I guess I sort of lost my temper.'

She shook her head. 'Boy, when you lose it you really do lose it. I hope this isn't the start of a new outlook on life—hitting first, thinking later.'

'It depends if anyone else upsets you,' he said, his blue eyes fixed on her.

'I don't need a protector, Jordan,' she retorted. 'I can take care of myself.'

'I know you can,' he said gently, 'but I'd rather like to be there with you, if you'll let me.'

She opened her mouth and then closed it again.

'What happened to your clothes?' she asked, deliberately changing the subject.

'Peter's orders, in case I decided to make a run for it.' He caught her eye and grinned. 'I'm completely starkers under here—want to take a look, inflame your female passions?'

'How can you joke at a time like this?' she protested. 'You're in serious trouble…'

The rest of what she had been about to say died in her throat as the cubicle curtains twitched open and an irate Peter Thornton appeared, with a huge piece of sticking plaster covering his nose.

'I am going to sue you for assault, Dr Marshall,' he exclaimed furiously. 'I am going to take you for every penny you've got!'

'Feel free,' Jordan replied dismissively.

'Don't be an idiot!' Claire snarled at him, and then fixed

Peter with what she hoped was a winning smile. 'I'm sure if we all calm down and talk about this rationally—'

'Rationally?' he exploded. 'I have been physically assaulted and my solicitor will be instructed to take legal proceedings against you forthwith.'

'Whatever you want, Pete, old chum,' Jordan replied.

'Are you insane?' Claire exclaimed, rounding on him. 'If you go to court your career will be ruined!'

He ran his tongue tentatively along the side of his mouth and winced. 'I don't care.'

'But, Jordan—'

'Claire,' he interrupted gently, 'don't you realise—even now—that you're more important to me than any career?'

She gazed down at him, her face a mixture of conflicting emotions.

'You'd do that for me?' she said, her throat constricted. 'You'd really throw away your career for me?'

He nodded, and when he suddenly smiled at her an answering smile crept to her own lips.

'Oh, very noble,' Peter said sarcastically. 'Very affecting. I'll see you in court, Dr Marshall.'

He swung round on his heel and Claire stepped forward, her face determined.

'Peter, if you sue Dr Marshall for assault I'll sue you for sexual harassment.'

He gazed at her in amazement and then shook his head. 'You wouldn't dare.'

'Try me.'

'Nobody would ever believe you,' he blustered.

Her eyebrows rose. 'No? I'm not the only female at the Ravelston who's had to put up with your wandering hands. There might be others brave enough to speak up too and, even if they don't, picture the headline—HEAD OF ADMINISTRATION IN SEX ROMP SCANDAL WITH INFERTILITY EXPERT—I reckon the board would have quite a lot to say about that, don't you think?'

For a long moment Peter said nothing. He just stared at

Claire, anger and fury blazing out of his eyes, and then he smiled with considerable difficulty.

'I think it might be better for the reputation of the hospital if we were all just to forget about this unfortunate incident.'

'That sounds very sensible,' Jordan said, 'but what about Claire?'

'What about Claire?' Peter demanded.

'I want you to return her resignation.'

'Jordan, I don't want it back,' Claire protested.

'Yes, you do,' he insisted, waving a hand at her. 'And you can tell the board, Peter, that I'll be happy to accept the position of head of the infertility clinic.'

'Are you out of your mind?' he protested. 'You can't honestly believe that I'd support you after what you've done?'

'It's the price of our silence, Peter.' Jordan smiled. 'Your price will undoubtedly be to make our lives hell from now on—but, hey, we can live with that.'

Peter all but ground his teeth. 'This is blackmail, Dr Marshall!'

'Isn't it, though?' he said, and laughed as Peter swung through the curtains in retreat.

For a moment Claire said nothing and then she cleared her throat.

'Jordan, it won't work—us, working together.'

'It will if we get something sorted out first,' he replied. 'Tell me why you came down to A and E, Claire.'

She stared down at the sheet covering him. 'Because I needed to know if you were going to be fit to work when I leave in four weeks.'

'And is that the only reason?'

'Jordan, I know what you're trying to do,' she began, 'but—'

'Claire, I'm too old for pride,' he said softly, reaching out and imprisoning her hand in his, 'but I'm not too old to beg. Won't you forgive me and marry me?'

'Sorry about the delay, Jordan,' Marian declared with a smile as she whisked open the curtains, 'but we'll have a porter along shortly to take you up to the ward.'

'You're keeping him in?' Claire said with concern. 'But I thought you said there was nothing wrong with him but a bloody nose and some bruising?'

'There isn't, as far as we can tell, but Dr Quentin would like him to stay in overnight for observation. Nothing's too good for our conquering hero.'

'You've got a fan there,' Claire said with a laugh as soon as Marian disappeared.

'I'd rather have you for a wife,' Jordan replied.

She sighed and shook her head. 'Oh, Jordan, I don't know…'

'You told me you loved me, remember?' he said gently. 'I know it seems like a lifetime ago, but you did say it and you said you'd marry me.'

'Jordan—'

'I see,' he said, his face suddenly a picture of indignant outrage. 'So you were just playing fast and loose with me, were you? Luring me into your bed with promises of marriage—'

'I never lured you anywhere!' she protested.

'And now…' He sighed deeply and hung his head. 'Now that you've had your wicked way with me, you're tossing me aside like an old boot.'

'I am not tossing you anywhere,' she exclaimed, starting to laugh, 'but, Jordan—'

'Claire, I love you. I want to marry you. Say yes—please?'

She did love him, she knew she did. Anne had said that it was just her pride that was standing in the way of her happiness and she knew that she was right. What did her pride matter? What did anything matter any more compared with the man who was gazing so fixedly at her?

'Take a chance on me, Claire,' he urged, as though he'd read her mind. 'I'm different now.'

'I'll say,' she said wryly. 'Hitting Peter, fighting with security guards.'

'Say yes, Claire,' he pressed. 'I promise you won't ever regret it.'

She didn't know whether she would or not, but she knew that she wanted to take that chance—oh, how much she wanted to take that chance.

'Before I answer you,' she said, her lips curving slightly, 'how do you feel about fatherhood?'

'Before or after we're married?' he asked.

She shrugged. 'I'm easy.'

'So that's what's written under your name in the gents' toilet,' he said thoughtfully. 'I've been trying to decipher it for weeks.'

'You're making that up!' she protested. 'I have never been easy in my life!'

'I'll second that.' He sighed ruefully. 'You're the hardest nut I've ever cracked.'

'A nut, am I?' she declared. 'I wasn't the one who put Peter in Intensive Care!'

He waved his hand dismissively. 'A broken nose and a bruise on his bum. Who knows? It might even improve him. Claire, will you marry me?'

Her eyes twinkled. 'I don't suppose you'd settle for us just living together again, would you?'

He shook his head. 'It's marriage or nothing.'

'Then it looks like I'm going to have to marry you,' she said.

He reached for her and pulled her into his arms, only to let out a yelp of pain.

'Hell and damnation,' he exclaimed. 'The girl of my dreams finally says yes and I can't even kiss her!'

'Life's a bummer, isn't it?' She chuckled.

'Maybe you could kiss my wounds better?' he suggested.

She leant forward and kissed his nose lightly. 'How's that?'

'That's not the only place it hurts,' he said plaintively.

She looked at him with concern. 'Where else does it hurt? Are you having trouble breathing?'

His blue eyes gleamed. 'Not yet, but I'm hoping to be very shortly.'

Her eyebrows rose questioningly and he pointed to the centre of his chest. 'It hurts a bit there, too.'

She shook her head at him and kissed his chest.

'And where it really, *really* hurts,' he continued, pulling down his sheet, 'is round about here.'

'I am not going to kiss you there,' she exclaimed, her lips twitching. 'What if somebody came in?'

'Claire, I'm a very sick man,' he protested.

'You can say that again,' she replied, her eyes dancing.

He sighed. 'And there was me thinking that you loved me.'

'Oh, poor diddums.' She chuckled, and obediently bent her head.

She didn't hear the curtains around his cubicle open but she certainly heard the shocked gasp that someone gave as they were quickly closed again.

'Who was that?' she asked, straightening fast, her cheeks scarlet.

'Sybil from the lab, bearing grapes,' he replied with an undeniable air of male smugness. 'She didn't stay. Must have got a shock or something.'

'Oh, *Jordan*!'

'I'd say you're definitely going to have to marry me now, don't you?' he observed, his lips curving.

And, as she began to laugh, she rather thought she would.

Your Special Christmas Gift

Three romance novels from Mills & Boon® to
unwind with at your leisure—
and a luxurious Le Jardin bath gelée to pamper
you and gently wash your cares away.

for just £5.99

Featuring
Carole Mortimer—Married by Christmas
Betty Neels—A Winter Love Story
Jo Leigh—One Wicked Night

MILLS & BOON®

Makes your Christmas time special

CHRISTMAS
Affairs

MORE THAN JUST KISSES UNDER THE MISTLETOE...

Enjoy three sparkling seasonal romances by your
favourite authors from

MILLS & BOON®
Presents™

HELEN BIANCHIN
For Anique, the season of goodwill has become...
The Seduction Season

SANDRA MARTON
Can Santa weave a spot of Christmas magic for Nick
and Holly in... *A Miracle on Christmas Eve?*

SHARON KENDRICK
Will Aleck and Clemmie have a... *Yuletide Reunion?*

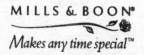

MILLS & BOON®

Makes any time special™

Available from 6th November 1998

SHANNON OCORK

SECRETS OF THE
TITANIC

**The voyage of the century
—where secrets, love and destiny collide.**

They were the richest of the rich, Rhode Island's
elite, their glittering jewels and polished manners
hiding tarnished secrets on a voyage that would
change their lives forever.

They had it all and everything to lose.

"Miss OCork is a natural writer and storyteller."
—New York Times Book Review

MIRA® Available from October 1998 in paperback

1-55166-401-1

FIND THE FRUIT!

How would you like to win a year's supply of Mills & Boon® Books—FREE! Well, if you know your fruit, then you're already one step ahead when it comes to completing this competition, because all the answers are fruit! Simply decipher the code to find the names of ten fruit, complete the coupon overleaf and send it to us by 30th April 1999. The first five correct entries will each win a year's subscription to the Mills & Boon series of their choice. What could be easier?

A	B	C	D	E	F	G	H	I
15					20			

J	K	L	M	N	O	P	Q	R
	25						5	

S	T	U	V	W	X	Y	Z
			10				

4	19	15	17	22

15	10	3	17	15	18	3

2	19	17	8	15	6	23	2	19

4	19	15	6

4	26	9	1

7	8	6	15	11	16	19	6	6	13

3	6	15	2	21	19

15	4	4	26	19

1	15	2	21	3

16	15	2	15	2	15

C8J

Please turn over for details of how to enter ➡

HOW TO ENTER

There are ten coded words listed overleaf, which when decoded each spell the name of a fruit. There is also a grid which contains each letter of the alphabet and a number has been provided under some of the letters. All you have to do, is complete the grid, by working out which number corresponds with each letter of the alphabet. When you have done this, you will be able to decipher the coded words to discover the names of the ten fruit! As you decipher each code, write the name of the fruit in the space provided, then fill in the coupon below, pop this page into an envelope and post it today. Don't forget you could win a year's supply of Mills & Boon® Books—you don't even need to pay for a stamp!

Mills & Boon Find the Fruit Competition
FREEPOST CN81, Croydon, Surrey, CR9 3WZ
EIRE readers: (please affix stamp) PO Box 4546, Dublin 24.

Please tick the series you would like to receive if you are one of the lucky winners

Presents™ ❏ Enchanted™ ❏ Medical Romance™ ❏
Historical Romance™ ❏ Temptation® ❏

Are you a Reader Service™ subscriber? Yes ❏ No ❏

Ms/Mrs/Miss/Mr ....Initials ....
(BLOCK CAPITALS PLEASE)

Surname..

Address ....

....

....Postcode.........................

(I am over 18 years of age)   C8J

THE PERVERSE PERSON'S

ABC

SALLY MALTBY

KYLE CATHIE LIMITED

First published in Great Britain in 1997 by
Kyle Cathie Limited,
20 Vauxhall Bridge Road,
London SW1V 2SA

ISBN 1 85626 270 7.

Reprographics by
Artwork, Southampton

Printed in Singapore

Sally Maltby is hereby identified as the author of this work in accordance with Section 77 of the Copyright, Designs and Patents Act 1988.

A Cataloguing in Publication record for this title is available from the British Library.

Lots of thanks to Caroline Taggart at Kyle Cathie for her advice and enthusiasm, and of course to Kyle for having been willing to publish.

and to Jenny and all at Artwork for invaluable technical support and advice.

and to Mary who first told me about this alphabet.

This book is for Reuben, Christian and Poppy, with love. Despite my enthusiasm, they remained sceptical throughout...

When I first heard and laughed at what has become known as the Cockney Alphabet I determined to make an illustrated book out of it. The differences between what we say and what someone else may hear seemed to give plenty of scope for visual interpretation. I have deliberately not added an explanation to most pages. The thing to remember is that some letters are capable of being pronounced two ways: they have a name, like Bee for B, and a phonetic sound, like the b in bug. It was also useful for my purposes that in colloquial speech the H is often dropped. Of course, none of this is to be taken too seriously: the truly fascinating thing about words is that you can say everything or nothing, be flattering or deeply insulting, sincere or deceptive, depending on emphasis and interpretation. This is surely subtle enough: only the truly Perverse Person would willingly indulge in the sort of confusion included here.

is for 'orses

It never rains but it pours
Every cloud has a silver lining

A virtuous woman's price is above rubies

DIAMONDS are a girls best friend

Ignorance is bliss

ANYTHING YOU LIKE IS EITHER
ILLEGAL, IMMORAL OR FATTENING

A little of what you fancy
does you good
(the two statements are not
necessarily mutually exclusive)

A word to the wise

in the subtle stew of
adages, maxims and proverbs
an aphorism is perhaps
distinguished by its
moral stance

a for

i s m

SLOW but SURE

He who hesitates is lost

MY CUP RUNNETH OVER
THERE'S NO GOOD CRYING OVER SPILT MILK

Procrastionation is the thief of time
Tomorrow is another day.....

B for

MUTTON

b for dark

C for SWIMMING

Could Covering a Corinthian Column Confound the Covetous?

C FOR TABLE

FER PAYMENT

Perhaps the cheque really is in the post....

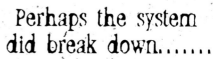

Perhaps the system did break down.......

Perhaps the accountant really has gone on holiday...

D

FOR

A

STATION

E *for*

DAM

329

PARADISE LOST.

To the subjected plain; then disappeared.
They, looking back, all the eastern side beheld
Of Paradise, so late their happy seat,
Waved over by that flaming brand; the gate
With dreadful faces thronged, and fiery arms.
Some natural tears they dropt, but wiped them soon;
The world was all before them, where to choose
Their place of rest, and Providence their guide:
They, hand in hand, with wandering steps and slow,
Through Eden took their solitary way.

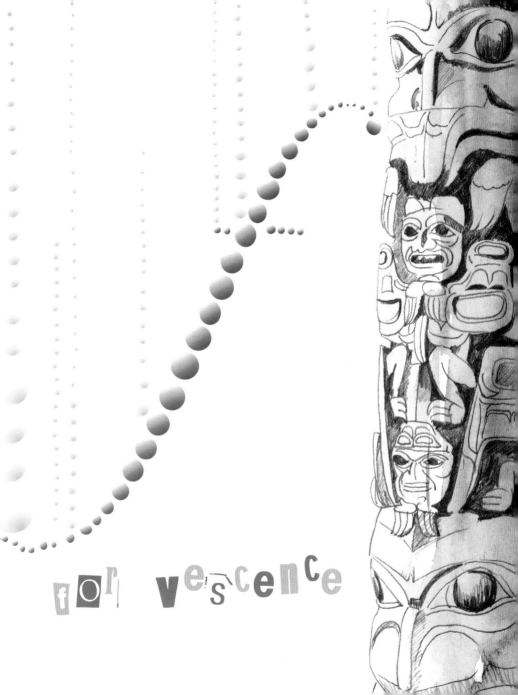

for vescence

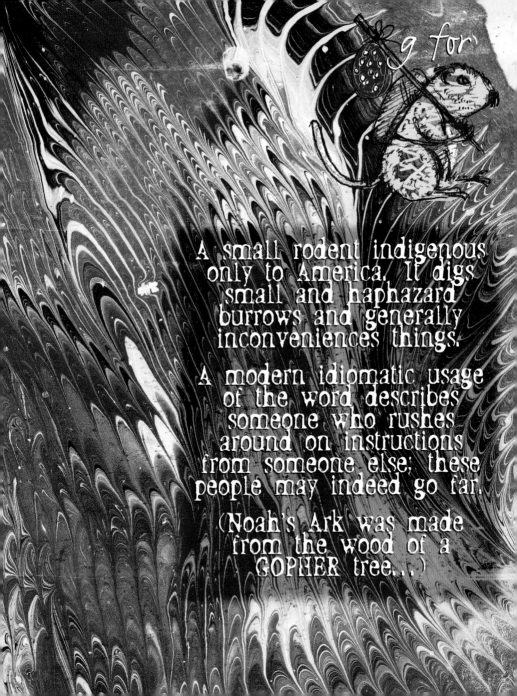

g for

A small rodent indigenous only to America. It digs small and haphazard burrows and generally inconveniences things.

A modern idiomatic usage of the word describes someone who rushes around on instructions from someone else; these people may indeed go far.

(Noah's Ark was made from the wood of a GOPHER tree...)

'NT MONUMENT

Ivory is the dentin which composes the incisor teeth or tusks of African elephants and the male Indian elephant. The teeth of narwhal, hippopotamus, walrus and sperm whale are also recognised as Ivory, but as they are smaller than elephant tusks they do not have the same potential use.

Ivory is a desirable material for carving, the creamy colour is widely admired, it is dense and durable and easily worked.

for ry

c d e f g a b c d e f g a b c d e f g

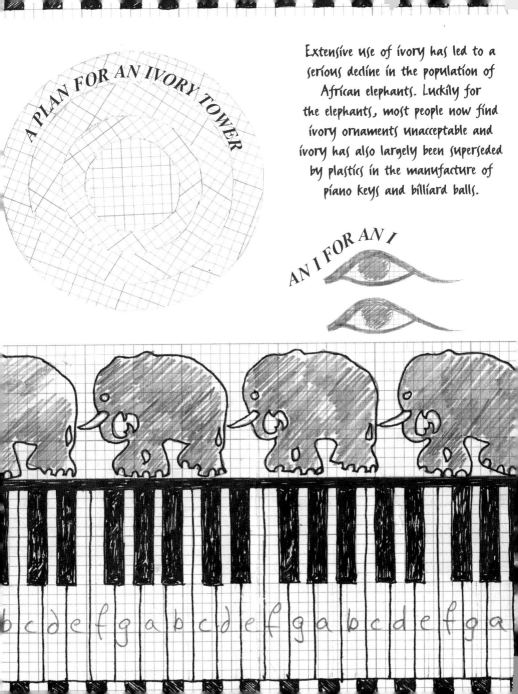

A PLAN FOR AN IVORY TOWER

Extensive use of ivory has led to a serious decline in the population of African elephants. Luckily for the elephants, most people now find ivory ornaments unacceptable and ivory has also largely been superseded by plastics in the manufacture of piano keys and billiard balls.

AN I FOR AN I

b c d e f g a b c d e f g a b c d e f g a

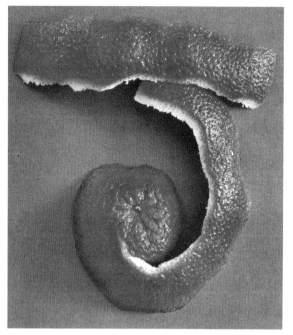

The word JAFFA became synonymous with oranges after commercial orange orchards were established at the beginning of the twentieth century near Tel Aviv ~ at Jaffa.

The name JAFFA has since been adopted by the Israeli citrus fruit marketing board as their trade~mark for all Israeli citrus fruit.

for ORANGE

Mandarin, Satsuma and Clementine are all varieties of Tangerine. Uglis, Ortaniques and Tangelos are hybrids produced from crossing various Citrus species.

Kumquats are not Citrus but Fortunella, although it is possible to produce hybrids between the two.

There are about eight basic
sorts of citrus fruit ~
Lemon Citrus limonum,
Lime Citrus aurantifolia,
Sweet Orange Citrus sinensis,
Sour Orange Citrus aurantium,
Tangerine Citrus reticulata,
Grapefruit Citrus paradisi,
Citron Citrus medica
and *Pomelo* Citrus grandis.

In spoken English the phrase 'Do you have..?' is often abbreviated to 'J'ave?' as in 'J for light?' and 'J for watch?'

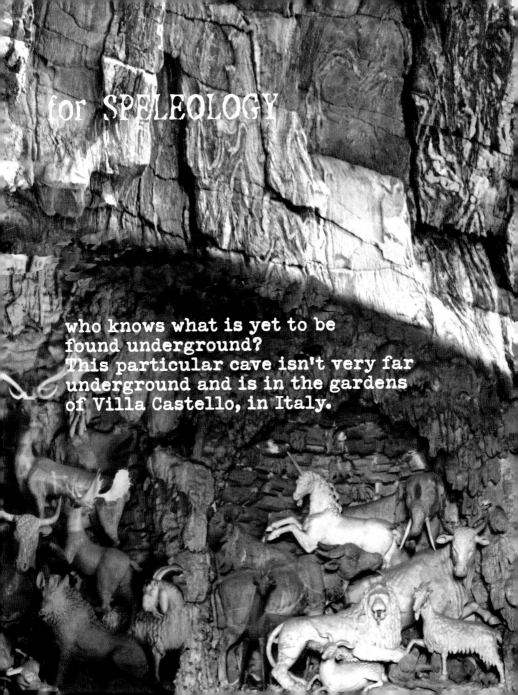

for SPELEOLOGY

who knows what is yet to be
found underground?
This particular cave isn't very far
underground and is in the gardens
of Villa Castello, in Italy.

for Bet

'L for leather

E F G H

abcdefghijklmnopqrstuvwxyz

M N

abcdefghijklm
nopqrstuvwxyz

P Q R

W X Y Z

just arrange the symbols above to make literature, philosophy, poetry and more day-to-day forms of human communications.

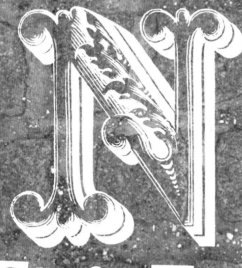

for cement

Vitruvius, in 'The Ten Books of Architecture', written around the 1st century BC, gives instructions for the building of city walls:- 'The towers should be set at intervals of not more than a bowshot apart, so that in case of an assault upon any one of them, the enemy may be repulsed with scorpiones and any other means of hurling missiles from the towers to the right and left....The towers themselves must be either round or polygonal. Square towers are sooner shattered by military engines, for the battering rams pound their angles to pieces; but in the case of round towers they can do no harm, being engaged, as it were, in driving wedges to their centre. The system of fortification by wall and towers may be made safest by the addition of earthen ramparts, for neither rams, nor mining, nor other engineering devices can do them any harm

RE-N FOR CEMENTS

O that I had wings
like a dove: for then
would I flee away and
be at rest.
PSALM 55 verse 6.

of a dove! & Far away, far a

which comes to much the same thing...

O for the hills and far away

e wings, for the wings of a dove!

Ernest Luff, who had an exceptionally pure treble voice, made the famous recording of the song 'O for the Wings of a Dove' in the early twentieth-century – it comes from Mendelssohn's oratorio 'O Hear My Prayer'.

In the

dim

p

for relief

For the bus

for and
the Knights of the Round Table.

There were, so it is said, around 150 Knights of the Round Table. The table itself was part of Guinevere's dowry and symbolised, by lack of seating precedence, equality. In most stories the Knights tend to be edited down to about a dozen.

Counting in dozens has obscure origins. Human beings typically have ten fingers and ten toes, so counting in tens or even twenties would seem obvious. A dozen is still used, in packing eggs for example, and hours, months, apostles and so on also occur in twelves. One explanation could be that 12 can be divided by 2, 3, 4 and 6, making it more practically useful than 10, which is divisible only by 5 and 2. And then there is half-a-dozen, a commonly used description for quantities, but never half-a-ten...

prit

From Duc de la Rochefoucauld (1613–1680):-
L'accent du pays ou l'on est né demeure dans l'esprit et dans le coeur comme dans le langage. (The accent of one's birthplace lingers in the mind and in the heart as it does in one's speech.)

The word *Sforzando*, to make a sudden emphasis in music, derives from *sforza* in Italian, meaning force. SFORZA was the appropriate name chosen by the cultured family that ruled Milan from around 1450 to 1535.

de corps & spirit d'equipe

In French the word *esprit* has lots of meanings:

a) Ghost or spirit, as in the Holy Spirit or 'to give up the ghost';

b) Wits or senses: *Perdre ses esprits* means to lose consciousness or to be prostrated by grief or misfortune;

c) Spirit in the chemical sense e.g. *esprit de sel* is hydrochloric acid and *esprit de bois* is methyl alcohol;

d) The intellect or mind, as opposed to the emotions: *Les grands esprits se rencontrent* means 'Great minds think alike';

e) Mood: *avoir de bon esprit* = 'to be in a good mood'; and best of all

f) *L'esprit de l'escalier* means literally 'Wit of the staircase', referring to all those clever rejoinders you think of after you have left the room or the moment has passed.

Which makes it all the odder that *esprit de corps* and *esprit d'équipe* should mean more or less the same thing – team spirit. In fact if you look *esprit de corps* up in a French dictionary it is likely not to be mentioned, though one dictionary I checked translates the French *esprit de corps* into English as 'esprit de corps', so maybe it was an English invention after all...

Tea is made from a plant related to camellias, though the term
'tea' also refers to an infusion made from
various other plant materials. The benefits of
drinking an infusion of the tea plant were
apparently discovered by the Chinese around 2700 BC.

for

two

It wasn't until 1517, when the Portuguese established trading
links with China, that the drink of tea was introduced into
Europe, and became increasingly popular.
The loss of flavour in stored tea is due mainly to its absorbing
water ~ which is the reason for foil~lining tea~chests. The word
caddy, used to describe a tea container, comes from a Malay
measure of weight, a kati, about 600g or 1 1/3 lb.

Like clothes,
euphemisms cover what we
really know is there, but we can't be quite
<u>sure</u> of the precise details. Saying that you want to
'powder your nose' or 'wash your hands' lends an element
of doubt to the situation ~ you might <u>just</u> want to do those
things, rather than perform the basic functions that persist in being
generally unmentionable. Similarly, if someone is said to have 'gone to a
better place' or 'passed over', it indicates that they might <u>just</u> possibly be
seen again.

All the euphemistic but politically correct statements involving 'challenged' e.g.
vertically challenged and follically challenged add an air of noble struggle to an
otherwise rather too final-sounding state ~ things just <u>might</u> change.
And to be 'let go' suggests that it was really you
who decided to leave, which probably isn't
true but the boss just <u>might</u> have thought
it was and it certainly sounds more
comfortable than being dismissed.
And then there are visual
euphemisms, like things to cover
toilet paper ~ the lady with frilly
skirts might <u>just</u> be an object
of interior decor, overlooking
the fact that everyone
would know precisely
where to look for
paper.

for culture

for
ESPAÑA

V

&

Viva Antoni Gaudi
(1852–1926) and Josep Maria Jujol
(1879–1949) both committed Catalan architects
working in a unique organic style. Gaudi's
grandest building, the Sagrada Familia
Cathedral in Barcelona, was conceived in
1883 and remains incomplete. Perhaps the
greatest achievement of twentieth–century
architecture will be finished in time for
the millennium?

The wonderful use of waste ceramic material on the extraordinary mosaic serpentine benches at Parc Guell, also in Barcelona, was largely the work of Jujol.

YOU Money

FOR BREAKFAST

OR THEY COULD BE:-
Sunnyside up - YOLK SHOWING, STILL A BIT GOOEY
Overeasy - TURNED OVER ON YOLK SIDE FOR I SECOND,
 NO MORE.
    Over medium - USE OVEREASY AS A GAUGE...
    Overwell   - " OVERMEDIUM   "
    Overhard   - " OVERWELL   "
Egg Pattie - PUNCTURE YOLK AND COOK YOLK SIDE DOWN,
OR PERHAPS BASTED, POACHED, OR SCRAMBLED (SOFT,
MEDIUM OR HARD, OR INDEED RAW), ON TOAST WITH BUTTER,
OR NOT, AND THEN AGAIN:-
OMELETTES, QUICHES, IN BRIOCHES, PANCAKES, FRENCH TOAST...

? ? ? ?

for

'*Strange to say what delight we married people have to see these poor fools decoyed into our condition.*'

Samuel Pepys

? ? ? ?

usband

'In married life three is company and two none.'
Oscar Wilde

Z for breezes

from Zephyrus, the god of the west wind, or the wind itself. In classical times the west wind was also called Favonius, the favourable wind. All the winds had descriptive names: 'Septentrio' refers to the seven stars of the Great Bear, seen in the northern sky; and 'Solanus' blew from the direction of the sunrise. Auster was an 'austere' wind from the south and Eurus took its name from 'aurora' for the dawn, etc.

Vitruvius (in The Ten Books of Architecture – see N page) understood the importance of accounting for prevailing winds when building a town:

'The town being fortified, the next step is the apportionment of house lots within the wall and the laying out of streets and alleys with regard to climatic conditions....

'For example, Mytilene in the island of Lesbos is a town built with magnificence and good taste, but its position shows a lack of foresight. In that community when the wind is south, the people fall ill; when it is northwest, it sets them coughing; with a north wind they do indeed recover but cannot stand about in the alleys and streets, owing to the severe cold....

'Some have held that there are only four winds: Solanus from due east; Auster from the south; Favonius from due west; Septentrio from the north. But more careful investigators tell us that there are eight.

Chief among such was Andronicus of Cyrrhus who in proof built the marble octagonal tower in Athens....

SEPTENTRIO
N

NW
CAURUS

NE
AQUILO

W
FAVONIUS

E
SOLANUS

SW
AFRICUS

SE
EURUS

S
AUSTER

Those who know names for very many winds will perhaps be surprised at our setting forth that there are only eight. Remembering, however, that Eratosthenes of Cyrene, employing mathematical theories and geometrical methods, discovered from the course of the sun, the shadows cast by an equinoctial gnomon and the inclination of the heaven that the circumference of the earth is two hundred and fifty-two thousand stadia, that is, thirty-one million five hundred thousand paces, and observing that an eighth part of this, occupied by a wind, is three million nine hundred and thirty-seven thousand five hundred paces, they should not be surprised to find that a single wind, ranging over so wide a field, is subject to shifts this way and that, leading to a variety of breezes.

z z z z z z z z z Z z Z z z Z Z Z z Z Z z Z z z Z

109

with all homage to
'MOTS D'HEURES: GOUSSES RAMES – The d'Antin
Manuscript' edited and annotated by Luis d'Antin Van
Rooten and published by Angus & Robertson in 1968

featuring
'the world's most famous omelette...' 'Un petit d'un
petit', and the immortal 'Pousse y gate, pousse y
gate...' – which just shows what you can do when you
take on another language...

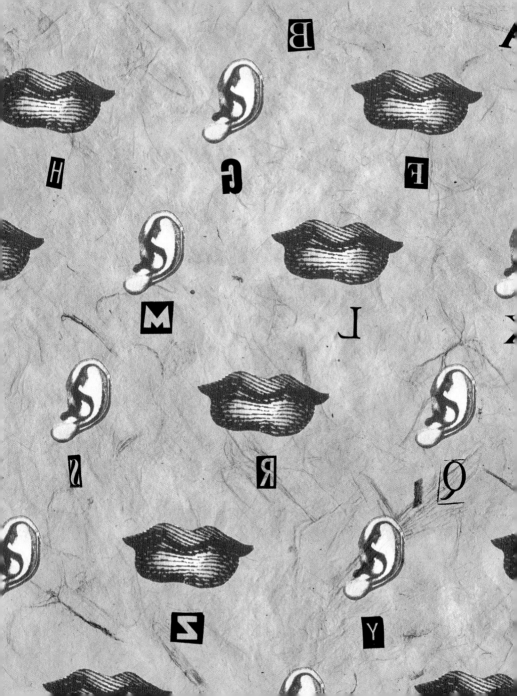